After We Left the Farm

After We Left the Farm by George H. Clowers, Jr. 2024

© 1998 The Moon Is My Confessor by George H. Clowers, Jr. Short Form

© 2015 Train to Tucker by George H. Clowers, Jr. Original Version

ALL RIGHTS RESERVED

This is a work of fiction. Any resemblance to actual events, or persons, living or dead, is entirely coincidental.

Cover Art by Deborah A. Clowers

The Moon Is My Confessor-Short
Train to Tucker-Long

There is a certain duality about life, and the older you get you appreciate that you played the hand you were dealt, and yes, sometimes, when it was your turn you dealt a card or two from the bottom of the deck. Well, let's move on to the stories.

The Moon Is My Confessor

I knew Downtown would be tough, but I didn't know I would have to kill a man, a man I saw standing on the corner, looking restless, and tired. I didn't think he would come after me, but he did, holding the knife by his side, cupped like a cigarette, and only a three-inch blade. I guess he just needed the dope and thought I was a dealer. When the police arrived, and asked me the first question, "Why were you here, boy?" I knew it would be a long night. This was a dope trap, and I was just passing through. They let me go after an hour and I went home to rest. Olivia met me at the door. She noticed the blood stains on my shirt but gave me a hug anyway. Nurses are like that. She didn't ask any questions and allowed me to get to the washroom to clean up, in silence. She brought me a fresh change of clothes and stood by my naked body. Her lips moved, but the words didn't come out. I finally gestured it was okay and she said, "Whatever happened, I'm glad you're home."

*

People never understood the ease with which I could put together a lecture. It was like play to me once the new theme of the semester was agreed upon. I would read whatever I wanted, change the office around a bit and maybe write out a short outline. When it was time for the first class I would watch the students arrive, post up at the lectern, and start talking. Usually they could listen for twelve minutes before someone would need to ask a question. That day it was Bryson.

"So, the intellect will go awry if not nurtured?" he asked, being sillier than usual.

"So, your question is, 'what happens to a silly man with a high IQ?'"

"That's right. Why am I in a philosophy class when I am a medical student?"

"Because you know medicine, but you don't know about choices yet," I answered him.

"Isn't that odd after six years of training?" he asked.

"It is, but why didn't you become a lawyer?"

Bryson paused, and looked around the room, especially focusing on Meyer Jacobson, his girlfriend for the past eight months. She had failed this class her freshman year and needed it now to finish her master's course work. She winked at him, then looked at me.

"I really don't have an answer for that one," he responded.

"Good, let's all turn to page 63 of the prepared text. Meyer, would you read for us?"

"Yes sir," she answered and begins reading after turning to the familiar passage.

*

After a brief discussion, I dismissed the class and called Olivia.

"Hey baby, what's up?" I ask.

"Nothing much. I just started a load of laundry. I meet Joan for lunch today at noon," she responds.

"Great, great, great. Look, that file I gave you last month to put away, where is it?"

"Taped underneath your middle desk drawer."

"Okay, good, thanks. I'll be home about two."

"I'll probably get back about that time as well. See you then."

"Okay, love you."

"Love you too."

*

It had been eight years, and the meeting was scheduled for 10 o'clock. Everyone would be there, my lawyers, their lawyers, the studio head, and the so-called writers of the script. I was very angry still after hearing them describe how simple it had been for them to steal my work, and the discussions about why they should not do right by me. My only solace was that the investors in the movie lost money, and the agent who gave them the story was crippled in a drive by shooting. The hearing today was to give me a check for 28 million dollars.

"Is everyone satisfied?" the arbiter asked, looking over to me first.

"Yes ma'am," I answered. She passed me the check.

"John, Rory, Paul?"

"Yes, we're done," the defendants answered.

"Okay, thanks to you all. This matter is closed."

Oddly, everyone was civil and shook hands. Lonnie Rivers, the principle writer, and secondary thief, nodded for me to meet him outside, and I did.

"I do owe you an apology. It was greed, and easy to present that a black man could not have written that type of story. I just wanted you to hear that from me."

"I appreciate that."

"Well, take care."

"You too, thanks."

He walked away as the others came out of the court room. No one else from their side looked at me as they passed by. My lawyers came up and thanked me. I had already given them their checks. Perhaps all this was behind me now and I could just be a college professor, I thought, until the phone rang, and someone warned, "Be careful. It's not over."

The next call was from Olivia who informed me that our house had been broken into, and the desk was overturned, and the file was missing. Nothing else in the house was touched. When I got home I viewed the relay feed. A man I knew did not know he was being filmed as he opened the file.

*

I thought back to the time I wrote that novella by hand, in 1998, it took me one month, June to July. It was the type of writing experience I had always hoped to have, gesturing, measuring, waking at 2,3 in the morning, writing what came to me from dreams, or actual events shaped to tell the story. It was quite a time and I fell in love with the rewriting, the editing, and the pride of having achieved a certain writing goal at the age of twenty-six. The story became a part of me. It was fun, even though it was a murder mystery. I guess, in a way, it prepared me for that night downtown when I had to react, and not think to survive. I could not let them just take that and get away with it. People had to pay for their wrongs.

*

"I'm great, what can I do for you today?" Lonnie answers.
"It's not what you can do for me, but what I can do for you," Dexter Oman boasts.
"I'm listening."
"I had a woman send me a manuscript her boyfriend wrote. They broke up, she's a druggie, and was looking to make some cash. It's a superb story, with great writing. It's good stuff, black stuff. You need to read it."
"How did she find you?"
"She said she found my name in a market book and read how I helped writers get paid."
"Have you paid her?"
"Yes."
"What do you want?"
"Read it, then we'll talk. I'm sure you'll be able to sell this one for some nice cash."
"Okay, send it to Franklin, regular mail. I'll tell him to look for it."
"Okay. I'll do it."
"Is it really that special?"

"It's really good. I know what still works today."
"Okay. Good."

CHAPTER TWO

It had been a large, sad funeral. Everybody knew Howard, whores, pimps, Opera lovers, patrons of the Symphony, auto workers, criminals, both federal and state, who had done time, and were still on probation. Though he lived alone, his legend was public. Myra was there, his ex-wife, dressed in those oversized diamonds he bought for her. Her cotton, full length black dress, and short brim pink hat, with the red ribbon, couldn't disguise her fear. They still were after her. Colette was there too, his girlfriend the past eight years, though dressed in a modest skirt, one could tell she'd lost weight recently. David Franklin was there too, in all his glory, crying more than the women, adding to speculation about the nature of his long-term friendship with Howard. Myra never trusted him during her six-year marriage to Howard, yet, had nothing out of the way to go on.

The gun shots rang out just before David fell to the floor of the church, his head bursting on three dark suited men with their sunglasses on. The echo in the Sanctuary added to the drama, and produced a chill, no, a tingle that spoke of irony, resentments, and love. The air stilled, and no one panicked, and all wanted to view who would move first, and where. Detective Harris, Howard's best friend from high school, not sober today either, didn't react to the second or third shots as they splintered the mahogany benches behind, and in front of Myra. No one else was hit. Then panic, screams, rustling feet, and laughter, 600 people beginning a slow stampede, light shoes, heavy shoes, expensive shoes, old shoes moved about at varying speeds. The carpet muffled most of the noise as the gunman, outside, walked to his car, tossed the rifle to the passenger seat, and drove down Meadows Street at 35 miles per hour, not looking back, not breathing heavily.

*

"The kitchen window works best in late summer," Howard thought to himself as he sat eating his breakfast of raisin bran cereal with milk, sausage, and a short stack of pancakes. It was 7am and bright, his full west view protected by white oak leaves and the overhang of pine needles that hovered just over the outer edge of the deck, with the red tips, at 22 feet tall, providing a wall such that he never thought to ask his neighbor to trim them lower. To the left and right the spaces between houses offered comfortable reassurance that, "we can leave each other alone, yet speak as we go about our lives." This being a corner lot, triangular and seemingly too far from people, Myra had never felt comfortable here, and when she left, she promised Howard Tatum that she would own a house where neighbors talked to one another, sat on the porch, took the time, and got to know one another.

Myra Jackson Tatum, 45, 5'3", 140 pounds of luscious attraction, with an innocent, almost angelic face, the kind of person doomed to failure, but who leaves a lasting impression, whether on your character defects, or your libido. To know her was to love her, but somehow you could never finish what was started with her but she lingered in your brain.

As Howard sat there, the day agreeing with his first cup of coffee, and a squirrel perched on the deck railing outside, looking back at him, he thought of the first time he made love to Myra. She met him at the door of her modest apartment, a somewhat musty odor salient despite the burning incense. She had refused three requests from him for her phone number, as one would do when approached on a bus. She gave in though after telling him she was laying low after so many dating failures the past year, but she was open to general conversation. He had called, and they became comfortable with what they talked about over a couple of months. Then, she had taken the risk of inviting him over.

Myra could feel herself moisten immediately, and Howard hardened. She smiled a wet look of acceptance, he smiled of conquest. She led him to a seat, as they both smiled on. The conversation wasn't awkward, nor rushed, and when he moved to kiss her she responded with passion. The bed was soft, her bra disappeared, his shorts were no longer, and he entered her with care. The juices flowed, a warmth unknown, a jerk, a stop, another kiss from the heart. Her grapefruit sized breasts delighted him so, his member a size she could bear. She guided him forward and back beyond, a pleasure intense, and raw with power. He humped and grabbed her, his weight now full, she smiled and sang a song of love, a choice, a fear, a soft refrain, "do it, do it, do it now!"

The squirrel moved, and Howard returned to present time, the phone rang, and he answered after the second notice, "Hello." A quick hang-up followed. This was the 15th in three days, and for some reason this one really unnerved him. The squirrel adroitly scampered away, Howard got up and poured another cup of coffee, and sat back at the window. Colette had bought him the round, hard pine table he used here in the eating area, though somewhat weathered from the month outside, it offered a rustic, mature something to the room.

Colette Hammond, tall, cultured, master's in counseling, though she works for Darwin Industries, a local phone service company. She and Howard share residences, but she won't marry him. She loves to get away to his house 30 miles east of the city, and he enjoys her loft downtown. When there, they can walk to dinner, the theater, or an opera, as they love to mix and mingle on their own terms. She, of course, enjoys the openness of Howard's half acre of land away from the city lights, and they both feel comfortable and at ease when together, and the relationship is solid.

*

The phone rang again in an hour, and Howard answered, "Hello."

"May I speak to Myra Tatum?" spoke a voice directly, and purposefully.

"She doesn't live here anymore."

"Is this Mr. Tatum?"

"Yes."

"I don't understand?"

"We divorced five years ago, and I haven't heard from her since," Howard responds.

"Mr. Tatum, Howard, is it?" she asks as though she knows all about him. "My name is Leslie Powell, and I am with T&F Collections, and we're trying to find your wife, ex-wife that is," spoken like a prison guard, with no affect.

He begins to feel a little curious, but doesn't really want to ask the obvious, next question, "What do you want with her?"

"Does she come there at all?" she further asks, rather curtly.

"No!" "Wait a minute," he thinks to himself after he responds.

"Mr. Tatum, I am authorized to offer you money if you can tell us where she can be reached."

"Excuse me, ma'am, I said earlier I haven't heard from her, well we divorced five years ago, but I haven't known where she is, or what she's doing in over four years. We talked some shortly after the divorce, but our split was abrupt and certain."

"Sir, our agency is trying to find her to retrieve an original manuscript by a David Franklin, a friend of yours I'm told. I can offer $250,000.00 if you can tell me where to find her."

The squirrel returns outside, looks at Howard a moment, and darts off. Several big, black birds are punching at fallen pears that lay scattered on the ground, down the hill, fifty feet back from the deck, close to the trees. Howard's interest is piqued now, but he maintains a poker player's calm.

"Mr. Tatum..."

"Give me your name again please, oh, I remember, Powell, Leslie," Howard jots it down on a slip of paper near the answering machine on the little black, oval table that sits in the corner, under where the phone hangs on the wall. "Phone number where I can reach you if I hear anything?"

"Nothing you can tell me now?" she asks him.

"Leslie, tell me about that manuscript?" he questions.

*

Howard, born and raised on the Westside of the city near Hunter Street, was 18 in 1971 when he began to shoot heroin. He did that for a year, went to rehabilitation, and never touched the stuff again, but made millions from 1973 to 1978 as a wholesaler of the product. He was never arrested, and no one witnessed any violent behavior by him. He remained modest, and people just thought that he got drunk and played horseshoes with his friends in the park. He rode public transportation, usually wore jeans, various sports type shirts appropriate to the season, and weather, and rotated name brand sneakers. He drove a small, older model pickup truck, dented in places, when he drove, and conducted business for only two hours a day.

Myra had met him on one such occasion when her boyfriend at the time, 'Old Folks,' had purchased three kilos. She thought they were there for money Howard owed Folks. The apartment was small, yet decently apportioned, felt comfortable, but one would not remember a thing about it, except maybe the abstract painting on one wall, its bright, yellow, and red streaks reminded her of what a womb looks like, the brief white and blue tints obvious.

She remembered Howard was cordial, but not too friendly. They had excused themselves and went into a back room as she sat on a blue and peach colored sofa, fringes of wear showing on the arms, yet quite a soothing seat. They returned, with Old Folks carrying a beige, cloth book bag, with two Gardenia blossoms spilling over the top, white with a tinge of pink color. They may have been cut from the bush yesterday. As goodbyes are said, Howard makes an appointment to see Folks in two weeks, on a Thursday night, about 8.

*

David Franklin was almost too good to be true, and people said that most of his life. He was not the best athlete on any team, but usually within your top three, not the best student in class, but in the top percentile, not the most handsome, or sexy, but you get the picture. Nature surely smiled on him. He was born on May 15, 1952, and had two older sisters. Even though he was the youngest, they were all treated equally, not spoiled, or pampered.

His parents were decent enough. His father was a waiter, a hyper-active, jolly fellow who earned good tips, and his mother was a part time fourth grade teacher. Their home was comfortable, with the usual arguments, and there was modest use of alcohol when the parents entertained. There was a high emphasis on educational pursuits, but not demanded. Everyone would follow their own path.

David met Howard when they attended Day Camp during the summer of 1962 and competed at ping pong. They both shared a memory of becoming physically close during swimming once and smiling. Neither mentioned it again.

*

"Franklin, Lonnie, what's up?"

"Not much."

"What do you think so far?"

"Interesting. I haven't read that much, but you know, it's pulling me forward."

"That's what I'm thinking. Not bad."

"I'll stay with it and see where it goes."

"Okay, we'll see."

*

Myra's dream had always been to be rich, and though Howard seemed to have just enough money for their needs, it was his verbal abuse that ran her off. She saved money, and spent reasonably, and though her bookkeeping job paid sufficiently it was just never enough for her. She worked extra and found ways to make money that Howard didn't know about, especially the year prior to their parting. She had become a consultant, socking away 14 grand, and when she met Mr. Cain, and he talked of making 'crazy money' with minimal effort, she was all ears. His offer to her was simple, she would come to work for him making $300,000.00 a year running his cabinet business and managing his other ventures. He would provide clients who had money, and she would handle the paperwork. He valued accuracy and discretion.

Mark Cain had done a 6-year bid for conspiracy to distribute cocaine, and the feds had known him for a long time. It had taken several arrests, and some guys who 'did what they had to do' to convict him. Cain was a character, slick as they come. When Myra went to work for him he had two years left 'on paper,' which she didn't know at the time. Cain's friends and business partners drove high end vehicles, and even the cabinet installers had custom vans and trucks. Most worked only one day a week.

*

"Myra, Myra, Myra," spoke Cain, striding into the office that Tuesday morning at 9, wearing a big smile, and a cool cap. "How are you this morning?"

"Fine. And You?"

"Good, good, good. Look, I need you to sign for a car I'm buying this afternoon. It will be delivered about 6."

"Sure. That means I get a two-hour lunch break, right?"

"Sure, sure; three if you need it. Just get back by six."

"All right."

"Oh, by the way, I need you to set up another bank account in your name for my new business, 'T-Shirt Heaven,' to start in two weeks. Use that new bank, Southern something, Southern Federal over on Luckie Street," he barks out to her in his haste to move on to the next thing on his busy schedule.

"Sure. Do you have someone for me to speak with there?" she asks him.

"No, just set up the account, put $20,000.00 in, and I'll tell you later."

With that he was gone, back out the door.

Cain drove a 5-year-old truck, with small dents about the body on the right side. He was dressed in a white, golf-type short sleeved shirt, with a little family crest on the left side, a red, white, and blue baseball cap with USA and the rings across the front that he had bought during the '96 Olympics in Atlanta. He wore well-worn jeans that were almost white, and a pair of season old sneakers. He had on his stainless-steel watch, and a half-carat ring he bought at a flea market for $200 dollars. The seller didn't know it was 80 years old, and worth fifteen thousand.

He stayed under the speed limit as he drove down Barker Street, parked in a lot for $8, and walked for 15 minutes towards the new basketball complex where he made the exchange with a rather nondescript fellow, then had to defend himself from a ticket scalper who thought he was muscling in on his territory. He walked back to the truck, got in, then had to get back out to give directions to a couple from Florida on how to get to the King Center, got back into the truck, and drove off, back to the office.

*

Myra had been with Mark for nine months now and had arranged the office to her liking. Though the furnishings were from an office rental place she had a good, supportive chair for her back, and the ten-foot-long desk made a slight, oval quarter turn that held her computer, keyboard, printer, and space for the other essentials. There were two leather, high back chairs for guests, though no one sat for long as Mark was prompt with his appointments.

As directed, she'd now signed for six cars, 2 houses, and jewelry worth $2.6 million. Although she had some unanswered questions, nothing seemed amiss. Mark had given her a $60,000.00 bonus for her excellent work, but the closer it got to 6, an indescribable fear began to grow within her, no, a type of dread like what she felt when she and Howard, years ago, visited one of his friends in the North Georgia Mountains near Ellijay. It should have been a pleasant experience, but something about the place had shaken her: the thick sound of the first part of the clear, rushing stream, eight feet wide, tumbling over rocks and mounds of earth, and the bird sounds, the foliage cover over head, made this a world unto itself with pure air, and streaks of sunlight touching on the vines and fallen trees, a deer stand, and a small campfire area close by.

Then, a special sense of terror that something or someone was watching, not to protect, but to observe and plot, then pounce perhaps, to destroy. Somehow the unfamiliar stillness betrayed the calm, and she had wished she were not there. The foreboding persisted as they walked deeper into the woods, ancient, and primal, with snakes, spiders, and other creatures around, in their natural habitat. She looked for bear tracks on the moist ground, which she couldn't really tell if she saw them. Her eyes darted all around this encasement, while the others seemed so relaxed, pacing themselves, enjoying the journey. Her heart raced faster as she wanted to flee, but to where? She wanted to tell Howard what she was feeling, but couldn't get the words out, as their gentle laughter and easy gait silenced her.

"Oh Mama!" she wanted to scream, "Please help me, Mama, help me please!"

As his hand landed on her shoulder she reacted in her rear end, a climax-type feeling, moistened by surprise. "Is this great, or what?" he asked, hugging her, but seeing a look of absolute horror in her eyes. It startled him, and he asked, "What's going on darling, you look dazed?"

"Help me," she replied, slowly coming loose of his grasp, sinking to the earth. Howard could break her fall somewhat, as Terri and John rushed closer to help.

She came to consciousness in a semi-private hospital room with no one in the other bed. The TV was off, and flower arrangements and cards were neatly placed about the window ledge. Fleetingly, she wondered where she was, before drifting back to sleep again. She was awakened at 7 by a nurse who said her doctor would see her now. "My doctor, miss, excuse me?"

The nurse turned abruptly away, studying the flowers, then responded.

"Oh, you've slept so, and I bet you don't remember much. Do you know where you are, and why?" "No."

"You're in Turner Medical Hospital. You were brought here to be assessed for a possible heart attack, but all your physical tests are okay."

Myra became aware of the slight pain under the small bandage over her left armpit, and a certain stickiness in about seven places on her torso, two near the heart, and two below, near her ankles.

"Now, as part of our complete services a psychiatrist will interview you."

She wanted to question, but instead asked if she could wash her face, brush her teeth, and fix her hair a bit. Just then, following a gentle tap on the door a man appeared.

"Good morning," he spoke directly to Myra. "I'm Dr. Gerald Cooper. Are you Mrs. Myra Tatum?"

"Yes, but..."

"I won't be long, nurse, thanks."

"He gestured to be allowed to sit in the chair next to the bed, and Myra nods yes. He sits.

***

At 5:45pm a tall, black man opened the office door and asked for Myra.

"I'm Myra," she responded pleasantly.

"Well good," he said nervously. "I'm Bobby, Mark wanted me to bring this car here. He said you'd sign for it."

"Oh yes, what kind is it?"

"A 1991 Luxury Four Door, wide side walls, beautiful."

He handed her a set of keys, she signed his triplicate form, keeping the top copy, then he left quickly, getting in a car driven by a 26 years-old woman.

Myra did the same thing each time, drive the car around the building to the dock where the installers picked up cabinets, and leave the keys on top of the right rear tire. It would not be there when she arrived for work the next day. Mark would come in, ask about the car, get the file with the white copy in it, and take it with him. No more would be said about the transaction, or where he kept the file.

*

This time, more than before, the call and quick hang-up unnerved Howard as he sat briefly on the couch in the den. He feared now that whoever it was may be getting frustrated and would act out in some way. He went upstairs, reached under the bed, and drew his 9mm with the de-cocker action, jacked it back, chambered a round and put it back. The phone rang again, and this time it was David.

"Howard, you've got to come quickly to my house, I need you in the worst way," he said breathlessly. "Someone has found out and they want me to tell them, they want the manuscript, now!"

That flushed sensation overcame Howard's body as he walked back downstairs and began pacing around the living room. At first, he wanted to run or jump up and down, or fight, or something! He decided not to do anything and told David that he was on his own. Just then the back door shattered, and three men burst through, armed with pistols, demanding he stand still. Howard complied, at first.

"Where is it, and don't lie?" said the lead intruder, big, and all business.

"What? Get out of my house, now!" Howard shouted angrily, as he moved for the steps to get upstairs. Big Boy grabbed him and tossed him to the floor. Howard jumped up quickly, pulled his knife from his back pocket, cut the guy in the groin area, spun around, dodged a bullet fired from the short man, kicked him in the groin area as well, spit on the third guy, punched his face, climbed the steps, secured his pistol, jumped down the steps, and shot them all dead, using five rounds from his 10-round clip. He surveyed the carnage, walked out the back door and called the cops. They arrived ten minutes later, inspected the scene, took Howard's statement, ruled self-defense, and let the body workers clean up the mess. Howard called the FBI the next day, moved into a hotel, and left town for a week. He had some moves to make.

*

Lonnie Rivers had worked with several agents in the past. He was not a script doctor but was good at picking the best parts of material, and fashion them into a creditable TV or movie work. He'd made a good living and could be honest about it if something had merit, or not.

This piece, however, was causing him some emotional strain, as some of his worst exploits from the drug days came to mind the more he read. Plus, he had some family of origin issues that were playing out in his head, and he couldn't understand why. A lot had happened up to this point, and he felt hooked by the story. He sent Franklin a text that he would read on, and for him to do the same. Franklin responded that he felt the same way.

*

David was having trouble keeping it together. Those urges were returning, and he couldn't fight them anymore. His body response was too compelling, everything shook, and pushed him in that direction. It was electrical, chemical, psychic, he had to give in to it!

It hit him as he passed the high school football field and saw a kid wearing his old jersey number, 31. The shrill panic startled him. He almost turned back, knowing something dreadful might happen, but he was powerless over his actions. He knew it was not like the old days, in the early '80s, when there were so many transients about that no one would know. Plus, they seemed fresher then, cleaner. You didn't think of diseases. He knew it was time again yet saw no one who fit the bill. He drove on, even going over to where the riffraff walked behind those dead looking prostitutes, but he could not imagine it happening with one of them, cigarettes bouncing from blistered lips, and twitching jaws. No, they would not do.

As he turned up Boulevard it hit him before he saw it, and he almost ran into a car on his right side. The pounce was on, even though he had gotten better at delaying gratification, he was ready now. He could enjoy the anticipatory moment and not rush. He moved his member back and forth, then held it, stroking gently, then rapidly a few times. He went slower again, easing his hands up and down, moisture, hot, warm, dripping, gravity laden on its path, moving, sweaty, soothing, before he knew it, he'd written another street scene poem.

***

The one question that gave Myra pause from Dr. Cooper was, "Had she felt suicidal within the past few weeks?"

"No," she answered emphatically, "although I feel Howard is about to ask for a divorce."

"Oh," responded the doctor, as if this were a profound response.

"Doc," she began, informally, "we've grown apart the past two years, it's just been sharing a house, and having sex. It's not been love for a long time. He's screamed it out of me, and I'm ready to move on," she said with a conviction that shook Dr. Cooper.

"Do you think what happened in the woods..." his head bowed as he read from the chart he held.

"Look, Howard has something some powerful people wish to obtain, and it's my fault. I stole, then sold a copy of something of his that's very valuable, and they want the original. I was stupid. They've threatened his life. The FBI is involved due to some of Howard's past life. I guess I've taken on some of that fear."

Dr. Cooper stared at her for a few moments, closed the chart, and said he would discharge her in an hour. He stood, pulled a business card from his shirt pocket, and told her, "If you ever feel the need to talk, or sort things out further, give the office a call and set an appointment. I'll be glad to work with you."

"Of course, doctor, thank you."

He placed the card in her left hand, shook the right one, and walked out the door. The nurse returned in 10 minutes and began the discharge process of papers to sign, and instructions to give. Myra was out of there in 45 minutes.

*

As questions and answers flowed, the FBI agents sensed Howard had a larger agenda. He had a reputation as someone to be taken seriously, and that all was not what it seemed with him.

"Okay," the female agent asked, "you kill three men in your house, and you don't know what they were after?"

"They mentioned a manuscript. Maybe it relates to the hang up calls I spoke about last week. I don't know. At any rate, it was scary."

"Three men?"

"Look, I got lucky. They were not that skilled."

"Anything else you want to tell us?"

"No, thanks for coming by. I feel better."

"Okay sir, stay out of trouble."

The agents left and called in a message for the duty officer to run a current background check on Mr. Tatum. Something was amiss here.

*

Mark called Myra on her cell phone at 7:45 am Monday, August 31, and asked that she not go to the office, but meet him at the Choose Us restaurant on Panola in 20 minutes. Mark drove a 2014 Black Luxury car today and Myra was in her triple white Elegant Sedan. The Choose Us morning crowd was made up of a retired couple in one booth pleasantly eating waffles, drinking coffee, and looking over the local morning paper; a young couple; four guys, workers for the county; and in another booth an older white woman and a somewhat younger black man laughing and joking away. They must be co-workers, or longtime friends.

Mark got there first and chose a booth in the corner farthest away from the register, yet directly facing the morning sunlight. The waitress came over and asked if he wanted coffee. He declined and said he was waiting on someone. "Water?" she asked.

"That'd be fine. Could you lower those blinds?"

"Oh yeah, sure, we usually do that by now, the sun's so bright this time of morning."

She moved away from the table, reached up and had a bit of trouble getting the blinds to drop evenly. Another waitress came over to help, and they got the two sets to come down together and closed them. Before they did, however, Mark could see Myra's car pull into the driveway. She joined him, smiling with a cheery, good morning face.

Myra was aging gracefully. She wore minimal makeup, exercised regularly, ate well, and her body was fit. She rarely mentioned aches and pains, even though she was 40% into menopause, with period flows decreasing, and some increase in sensitivity and restlessness some days.

Her business and social duties were not hindered in the least, and she went about her affairs without much fanfare.

Mark was a regular customer here and when the waitress returned he ordered his usual breakfast of grits, a waffle, eggs, and crispy toast. Myra thought that a bit much but wanted a little of each, so she ordered the same, with coffee. Mark ordered orange juice with his, telling the waitress, "Coffee later, maybe, thank you."

Mark got right to the point of this meeting. "Your, that is, the six cars are missing," he said bluntly.

"Missing?" Myra quizzed. "My cars, what do you mean?"

"The cars you signed for. I leased them out to some people and now I can't find them, the cars, or the people. One by one they've disappeared!"

"Mark, what are you telling me?" asked Myra innocently yet knowing. Her instincts had told her something was wrong, but the money was so good she allowed herself to disbelieve what was going on.

"You, or rather, we have to find them soon."

"Mark, tell me you're lying, those were not my cars, I just signed…"

"You got it."

"Oh, my God," Myra whispered under her breath.

"Another thing, everybody has to move out of the houses."

"Mark, no, no, don't tell me! What have you done to me?"

"Well, it was supposed…"

"Mark!"

"Okay, bitch, don't push me. You're no schoolgirl. You knew what was up," he said angrily, and somewhat menacingly.

Myra wanted to slap him, or go pee, or something. She became very confused, and disoriented, and didn't notice that the waitress had placed their food on the table, poured more coffee for her, and asked Mark if he was ready for a cup.

"No thanks," he replied. "Check back in a few minutes and get me another glass of juice, large," he commanded.

Myra thought back to some of the arguments she and Howard would have, how she couldn't believe the intensity of some of his expressions of anger over everyday matters. How he never learned to fight fairly with her, as if there would be no reconciliation. He just had to be right all the time.

She cut her waffle in half, mixed the scrambled eggs and grits, and buttered the waffle halves. She cut the two pieces of sausage into fourths, not remembering that the order was for bacon, poured syrup over the waffle half closer to her, and began eating without a word. She and Mark played eye tag sporadically. The waitress brought Mark's juice and coffee, set them near his plate, and asked if everything was okay. Mark and Myra said "Fine," in unison, and laughed nervously.

*

Mark Cain's mother had been sickly the past couple of years, and when he came to visit he would spend an hour listening to her reminisce about his father and what a good man he was. She'd question him about his work and hoped he would not go back to prison. She knew he was a conniving type, and she didn't trust him, but he faithfully came by once a week. She was past preaching to him and hoped he would straighten out on his own.

His facial expressions were like his father's, bright and earnest, with a hopeful smile, but while his father used them to inspire, Mark used them to cheat. Privately, his latest scheme had him worried; things had gone very wrong. Few people trusted him now-a-days, cash was tight, and the financial institutions were calling him in about missed payments. He needed to shift the blame, and Myra would have to take the fall, he didn't want to go back to prison. Even though federal time is not hard to do, everything about the loss of freedom was freaking him out.

As he drove towards David's house, he became more restless. David was a different kind of crook, and not a real criminal. Myra had been angry back then, and now regretted what she had done. David had simply become a pawn for them, a legal front that Myra didn't know about. Mark had not told her everything he was doing. She had no idea about the consequences of her actions.

*

Wedgewood was a blue-collar area of town, low middle, yet everybody respected the struggle. If Jimmy's daddy were a drunk, the kids still called him Mr. Davis, and if somebody's family got surplus cheese, there would be jokes, but they were still your friends. People worked together, and helped one another, but not in an embarrassing way. If Danny Lee worked, gambled, and spent all his money on the weekend his mother would get after him, but he would still have a place to stay; it wouldn't even come up to kick him out. He'd leave on his own one day, straighten out, get married and settle down by the age of 27. Church would be talked about, and strongly recommended by the older relatives, who in some cases had done the same things. Aunt Lucy, of course, would tell you, "You need God."

Myra grew up just below this attitude. People who got drunk got ridiculed. Gamblers slept in hotels, and loose women usually had fat, puffy eyes on Sunday morning. She saw this growing up, and somewhere around 12 or 13 vowed to live better and right, marry a good man, have a house, and go to church. She would dream of this often, as years went by, until Old Folks came back from Vietnam in 1970. Somehow everything changed then, and she found herself in night clubs dancing and sleeping around, getting drunk on the weekends, and moving in with Thomas, unmarried. He promised to marry her, but never did, of course. Though their four years together had some glamour and suspense, and he fulfilled her sexually, he was not the type of man she wanted to spend her life with. When he died, she moved across town to Dublin Street, and ran into Howard Tatum a few times, and he finally spoke to her.

"Hey there, don't I know you?" he asked, moving closer to her as she walked from the bus stop.

"I don't think so," she responded with caution.

"Folks, Thomas Holmes, weren't you his lady?"

"Oh yeah, I remember you. What's your name?"

"Howard. Howard Tatum. And yours?"

"Myra Jackson."

"Do you live around here now?" he asked her.

"Yes, for about a month now, over there on Dublin Street." She pointed to a decent, 8-unit apartment building just up the hill, which Howard owned.

"Oh good, good, that's a good place," he shared.

"And you?" she asked him.

"Not far from here, but I spend a lot of time around here. I know people here, I sort of grew up here," he said to her.

Myra began to feel aroused, not sexually, well yeah, but more as in alive, or enlivened. Howard too felt jolted by that certain something that pulses through the stomach when something special happens.

"Well, I'll see you around," spoke Myra as she started walking for home.

"Okay, take care, see you around," Howard spoke back to her.

*

The night Howard's brother was killed, it was raining. The accident happened on I-20 near the ramp for 75-North. The brown 1967 car sideswiped him, and Aaron's car hydroplaned two lanes, missing an old couple in a pick-up truck, and slid off the shoulder down a 15-foot embankment. He was dead on arrival at Grady Hospital, a half-mile away. The EMT ambulance was there in 8 minutes, but it was still too late to save him.

This is when Howard stopped shooting heroin and stayed buzzed on 'Mad Dog' for about six months. He loved the way that cheap wine warmed his body, like the way he felt with certain women. Even though Aaron was older, Howard felt protective of him, and wished he had been with him that night, thinking that maybe he could have saved him. Howard loved his brother, and cursed God often for his death. Yet, years later, when the Olympics came to Atlanta, and Howard was up at 6am, walking up old Hunter Street, now Martin Luther King, Jr. Drive, he thought how wonderful it was to have this incredible event in their 'backyard', and thanked God for the spirit Aaron had left him, how competitive and equally matched they were growing up. Aaron was smart and articulate and had a 'can-do' will and spirit that was inspiring to all who knew him.

Howard thought of the time when they were about 12, and he slapped Aaron after a game of horseshoes. Aaron chased him to their grandmother's house shouting, "Come here!" and had a confused look of rage on his face, and how he had felt like he was running for his life, how he hadn't known why he hit him, but knew he had to run for safety.

Howard had snatched the wooden screen door open, rushed through the living room, and found Grandma standing in the kitchen. Aaron followed a few seconds later, and she held him off from Howard.

"What's wrong?" she asked them. Aaron explained they'd been playing when Howard slapped him.

"Ahhh, he didn't mean it," she kindly offered. "Y'all quit playing so rough." She hugged them both, and nothing more was made of the incident.

*

The two men had followed Mark for 40 miles now, out I-20 East past Shady Dale. When he noticed the tail, he doubled back through Newborn, and on to Rutledge, then came back up 20 going west. They stayed with him, never getting closer than fifty yards. Mark called Myra, told her to find Larry, and have him come to the office in 20 minutes.

She found him at Nate's Barber Shop, and he said it would be about half an hour before he could get away. Myra called Mark back, told him the time frame, and he said okay. By this time, Mark had identified the Hunter Green car as the one Toby Matthews drives. He'd been avoiding Toby for a week because of the $40,000.00 he owed him. Toby was a street fighter and had beat Mark up before, about a year ago, over a similar debt. Mark couldn't quite make out who was with him, but thought maybe it was Warren Gifford, an old dope fiend from Wedgewood. Mark had gotten Warren's sister Laura pregnant in high school, and the abortion had been a problem. Warren had never forgiven him for all that, and generally didn't like him.

Mark drove on to the Panola Road exit, went up and came back around, got back on 20 and saw Larry's car passing by him at 80 miles an hour. Larry took the Gresham exit, and Mark went on up to Glenwood to give Larry time to get back to the office parking lot. Larry parked a few spaces from the office door, hesitated long enough to let Toby park near him, stayed in his car, and nodded to Mark, signaling he had his '9' ready. Toby spoke first.

"What's up, my brother?"

"You got it, your world," said Mark. "What's up Warren?"

"Don't!" said Warren, fiercely.

"You got my money?" Toby shouted.

"Hold up man, keep it down," Mark requested.

Just then Myra came out the office door and told Mark he had a phone call. He acknowledged her, holding up a finger to signal "Give me a minute."

"Toby," Mark began, "Let me give you $8,000.00 now, and the rest tomorrow by noon."

As Mark was speaking they all heard Larry jacking back the slide of the 9mm auto-loading pistol, as he moved from his crouched position beside Myra's car.

"Well damn!" said Toby, recognizing Larry. "Well I'll be God-damned, Mark, you bastard!"

"Larry, put that away," spoke Mark to his friend. "Toby, come on into the office, I might have 12. I'll give you the rest tomorrow."

Toby nodded, and they went in. Larry relaxed and put the weapon away. Warren sat back in the car, leaving the door slightly open.

*

Sure, David knew Mark was trouble, but they'd made money together on several occasions. David hadn't wanted to know details before, but now Mark was involving Howard by way of Myra's misdeeds. Mark found out about the manuscript, and what Myra had done, and tried to squeeze some money from her, and even contacted one of the studio heads trying to con his way into a payoff. David and Howard were too close, and Mark didn't understand true friendship.

*

The plan had been simple, Myra photocopied a novella with poems handwritten by Howard years ago and sent them to a New York based literary agent. The agent, and two writer friends mined several ideas, and sold them to film producers where two movies, a novel, and a TV series were birthed. Myra pulled David into the deal, and they were paid a handsome sum. A crooked studio head wanted the original because now, two years later, an anonymous author claimed he wrote the work, and had filed a lawsuit implicating at least six people involved in the conspiracy. Deals were brokered, careers threatened, and millions of dollars were at stake, as well as the integrity of certain people who were drawn into the mess unaware of the issues involved. Oddly, it was Larry who found out about the deception, so when the physical threats began, David had gone to Howard and told him all about what had happened. Myra and Mark didn't know this, and

Howard never let on that he knew. When the calls and hang-ups started, Howard set a trap to catch the perpetrators. He didn't care about the money, or potential for fame, he was just really angry that someone claimed his work as their own.

*

David knew Howard would never give up the original manuscript, and he wasn't sure who this anonymous author was, and what backup they had, but he knew he was on his own now. Mark and Myra were just thieves, and didn't have any investment in anything, so agreeing to meet Mark tonight was unsettling, but had to be done.

Hamilton Park, located in a good neighborhood, was small, about 60 acres, maybe. It had picnic tables and grilles, large and small pavilions, a softball field, and tennis courts. In past years, as it had become run down, the drunks, transvestites, and general 'night owls' used it for various deeds. Now it was lovely again, well-kept, and popular for family outings, and a vigorous softball league. The City Councilwoman for this area had grown up here, and knew, when elected, she'd better deliver, and had. The older residents could come out to walk the grounds or sit and enjoy the area again. No bodies had been found in the last three years.

David had agreed to meet Mark about 7pm, just before twilight. Mark arrived first, parking near a small gathering of teenagers hanging out in one of the smaller pavilions. He noticed the beers, but they were not loud, or boisterous, but clearly too young to be drinking.

He sprang from his truck and began pacing around. When David showed up about ten minutes later, his car slowed down, but didn't stop. Someone from the back of the car fired three rounds, and Mark fell to the ground, his chest torn apart. The teens dropped their beers and ran. Mark died alone, on the sidewalk.

*

Howard became more bewildered at the hang up calls. Myra did not live with him, and, if they were doing any actual surveillance they would know she had not crossed that threshold in a long time. The number was not traceable by the normal system offered by the phone company, and he didn't want to hire an attorney, nor did he want a private number. He called the FBI back, but they were no help, so he was glad to get that call from Doug. Howard understood systematic torture, harassment, and wearing a person down; he had done that to Myra. It was not intentional, but the actions of a selfish, immature man. He had to admit to himself that he was afraid of what might happen, his sense of security was threatened. This had been going on for two years, it was time for it to end!

*

Larry was an odd fellow, crude, dangerous, yet he enjoyed his Thursday evening pinochle game with the old ladies at the Assisted Living Home. He would be on good behavior, and they enjoyed his strength. He didn't tell those dirty jokes anymore, and they were glad. The conversation was always interesting. One night, Margaret Hannah, after she beat Thelma's king with a ten, mentioned her son Ronald, the movie producer, and how well he was doing in Los Angeles. She went on about how he got his start in the publishing field, had worked on two books by a new author that became best sellers, and then moved on to writing scripts for TV movies, 'Please Don't Bury Me in the Rain' being the biggest hit, and how he now produced movies for himself. She indiscreetly mentioned he had made over $40 million the last two years with rights, royalties, and some other things she couldn't remember. Larry oohed and awed like Thelma and Sara at the appropriate times and made a mental note to call Howard. The books and movies she described sounded like that little book he had read of Howard's years ago, and that David and Myra had done something crooked with. When Larry got home he called Doug, and they talked for about 20 minutes.

*

Larry, who'd agreed to fly to L.A. the next week, was surprised to sit next to David on his return flight. David spoke first.

"Larry, what's going on; I'm surprised to see you out here?"

"Hey David. What's up is a short visit to my sister's house in South Central. What's up with you?" Larry asks him.

"A deal I'm working on," is David's crisp reply.

"Movies?"

"I'm out of that; don't start."

"Does your probation officer know?"

"I'm off paper; no monthly reports, nothing. I'm a free man again," spoken with a bit of pride.

"Loose is more like it."

"Don't start that. Can we be friends again?"

"I'm just still angry about how you and Myra crossed out Howard like that."

"I know. Looking back at it we were really stupid."

They both notice cuts on the other's fingers, but don't comment. Larry's thumb is bleeding just a little bit from hitting up against the metal seat frame as he sat down. David tries to hide his injuries.

*

Ron Hannah lived in Marina Del Rey, about 20 minutes from Second Avenue. The lawns were bigger, and the houses three times as large. Ron and Sheila had bought here, paid $330,000.00 for their cottage, put a quarter of a million into it, and had it laid out nicely. Sheila liked the area because it was near her parent's house, and Ron had a short commute to the studio. It was a lovely area with palms, bright flowers, and the ocean nearby. Sheila was out of town the night Ron was murdered.

"Yes, who is it?" Ron asked as he got to the front door and opened it before he heard the response. The killer pushed him back into the house, pulled out a knife, and tried to slash his throat. Ron twisted away, ran to the kitchen, and grabbed a water glass, cracked it against the granite countertop, and threw it at the attacker. The killer held up his right hand to deflect it, but sustained cuts to his fingers and thumb, which angered him more. He rushed to grab Ron, hit him twice in the stomach, and pulled out a pistol and shot him in the head. Ronald Hannah dropped to the floor, lifelessly.

The killer went to another room, unzipped his pants, and, breathing heavily, relieved himself from the heightened state of arousal. After the initial burst semen slowly dripped over his fingers, and he stood there a moment looking skyward, and exhaled, as if emitting cigarette smoke. "Ooh Baby," he thought. Sticky, he pushed himself back into his underwear, paused a minute, zipped up, and strolled back out through the house, and just missed getting blood on the bottoms of his shoes. He closed the door gently, looked around as he walked to the sidewalk, and disappeared in the dark and hanging foliage.

*

Knowing Ron Hannah's death was no accident, the group became concerned. Lawrence Stevens, the private detective they hired, was out and about getting the police report and whatever else he could find out from the streets. Paul Taylor, head of Hoffman Publishers, John Palmer, head of Tantamount Pictures, and Rory Horton, CEO of Canyon, House, and Berger Investments were meeting to discuss how, if at all, Ron's death affected their operations.

"Are the hang up calls still being made to Mr. Tatum?" Paul asked.

"No," Rory answered quickly.

"Obviously, we didn't shake him?" Paul asked out loud.

"No, as a matter of fact, my friend at the Tech Center found out how he broke the phone block, and found the originating number, so we closed it down. He almost scared John's son to death when he showed up in the parking lot that afternoon," Rory said directly to Paul.

"That's right," offered Mr. Palmer, sitting quietly off to one side of the room. "He's still not ready to come back to the states. His therapy is going well, but he does not want to work for us again. The doctor isn't sure if he'll be able to work, or finish school any time soon. He's in a stupor, like someone on tranquilizers."

"John, I'm sorry," Paul spoke. "What exactly did Howard do to your son? You should have told me while I was in Japan."

"He made John Jr. sit in the car with him and listen to the 231 hang up calls the computer made to his house phone. When John tried to escape, Howard 'accidentally' broke his jaw, and left hand. He's only 19," said John.

"Tragic. All right, what do we do now?" asked Rory.

"We ought to drop it. We'll never get the original now," said John.

"I've got one more angle," offered Paul, "and if it doesn't work, we'll forget it. I hear from David that Howard has another book, equally as good."

"Oh, come now," replied Rory, "that thief! No way! Why should we do business with him again?"

"I'm leaving," said John. "I've got movies to put on, not conspiracies to be a part of."

"Now you're a moralist?" shot Paul.

"Not so much, but I've got a son to see about, and possibly find a little integrity again. This has been bad."

"Oh well, let's keep in touch," offered Rory. They all left the room and went their separate ways.

*

The killer sat in his small, furnished efficiency, battling intrusive thoughts about "Ginger," who was she? His swollen hand was healing, and the small cuts were barely noticeable now. His head throbbed occasionally, and his back ached at times, but the ibuprofen helped; he'd even thought of a shot of heroin, but quickly nixed that idea. The pains would go away.

*

Myra had placed her diamonds in a safe deposit box before going to prison and thought to get them out now that she was leaving the women's shelter. The transition had gone well, and she needed to buy furnishings for her apartment. She could continue using public transportation to get to work and all but would eventually need a car. She thought to call Howard and ask for a few thousand but rejected the idea the first few times it came up. Soon though, she found herself dialing his number. He answered on the first ring.

"Hello."

"Howard, hey. This is Myra."

"Hey, how are you?"

"Good, good, look, I've just moved from the women's shelter into an apartment over on Shallowford Road, and I need to get a few things. I've been working at Yo-Mart, and have some money saved, but I could use some help."

"How was prison?" he asked her.

"Not bad. Federal people usually have money, so you don't have to deal with certain types of foolishness. I can't say it was fun, but I got through it okay."

"What would help?" he asked.

"6, 7 thousand. You know, washer, dryer, fridge, a few other things. A car at some point. A little reserve, you know."

"How about 10?"

"That'd be fine."

"Shall I mail it, or...?"

"No I'll come get it. Look, Howard, I'm sorry."

"I know, forget about it. Lessons."

"Yeah, but I was so stupid. I'm sorry."

"Okay, I'll be here until Monday; then I fly up to Cape Cod."

"How about if I meet you for lunch downtown tomorrow; I'm off on Fridays?"

"That works. Tommy's on Luckie Street, about 11:30?"

"I'll see you then," she responded.

Howard and Colette had tickets for La Boheme at the Fox next Saturday night. It was a production by an Australian Troupe whose performances had been billed as sensitive and quite good. Colette had viewed a Laser Disc recording and agreed with the assessment offered in the flyer.

*

David wasn't sure what he wanted to do now. Running into Larry in Los Angeles had changed some of his plans. With about $200,000.00 stacked he thought of maybe leaving Atlanta, and living somewhere else for a time, get a job, read books, and just relax. Feeling lonelier than usual, he wished he had a partner. He was jealous of Howard and Colette's relationship but was happy they were together.

David had never quite been able to be intimate for long periods of time. He didn't connect on a deep level somehow. People liked him, he was smart, but he just didn't seem to fit with anyone. He figured he'd better drop any illegal plans he had and stay legit. He was, however, feeling a bit frisky today, and thought maybe he'd go to Paradise City, have a few drinks, spend a little money on the dancers, and get a prostitute for the night. "Well, maybe?" he thought, just before the phone rang.

"David, hey, it's Paul Taylor. You were hard to find!"

"Paul Taylor. I didn't think I'd ever hear from you again."

"Well look…"

"Paul, the answer is no, before you start," David said to him, and hung up the phone.

Howard had decided to give the original manuscript to Nichols College in North Point. It was a small liberal arts school founded eight years ago, by retired Atlanta Public schoolteachers, with faculty from around the world. Howard had been a consistent financial supporter and hoped this donation would at least add to the endowment.

*

After Howard's funeral, the killer flew out to Colorado, killed Franklin Byrd and Lonnie Rivers, then flew to Los Angeles to put Dexter Oman out of his misery. A month later I wrapped up the fall semester with a lecture on Honesty.

Train To Tucker

Bethany Richards first met Vincent Edwards at a house party thrown by Susie and Mark Davis to celebrate the fifth anniversary of the opening of their café' on Hardee Street. Susie and Beth were friends from school, and Vincent was a regular at the café.' He was always friendly and nice when he came in for coffee, and to sit in the TV room. Plus, he was new to the area and single, and Susie invited him to meet Beth, and for them to maybe hit it off. He was gregarious and wonderful as he met everybody but had given Beth a simple 'How are you?' when he walked past her. As the evening progressed, and the dancing started, Beth saw him standing alone and asked him to dance. He agreed, and their moves seemed to come together immediately. They talked, danced with others and before leaving about eleven he asked for a phone number. She gave it to him, saying, "Coffee soon?"

"Sure," he had answered.

Vince thanked Mark and Susie for inviting him over and waved to Beth as he was leaving.

"Handsome," Beth commented to Susie later heading up to the guest bedroom.

"Who?" Susie asked her.

"The guy, Vincent, you know, big smile, fun loving," she answers.

"The writer?"

"Oh, is he a writer?"

"Yeah, Poet I think he said, teaches at the community college."

"Wow, that's great."

"You have some interest?"

"We danced a bit, and he asked for my number. He seemed nice enough."

"He's always friendly when he comes in to the store."

"Alone?"

"Best I can tell."

"Okay. We'll see. Good night."

"Goodnight darling. We'll see you in the morning. Thanks for staying over."

"Sure, great, great party."

*

Vince almost threw out Beth's phone number before Monday's first class. He had on the same pants he wore to the party but had forgotten he had it. He had thought about her briefly since then, and the party, "It was fun," he thought.

*

Today's talk will be about structure and how each poet should find the usages that work for them. He was not formal in his syllable count but when he heard the music, that's when he knew it was working.

"Have you ever used formal structure?" a female student asked.

"Consciously, about 20% of the time. My formal training was limited, so I just wrote what seemed right to me. In high school, I learned the basics, and so have you. And part of your grade for this semester will be to show that you know the definitions. They are important and we will probably spend about two days on nothing but that, and I'll warn you ahead of time. As a precursor to that let's get this on the board and you can follow along on your device and make notes. Let's see what I did consciously, and what just flowed from the unconscious, or rather, innate ability."

Let's Keep What We Have
Let's keep what we have,
The honest feelings, frankness with tact,
Your soothing words are like a salve,
Healing my wounds, as if by contact.

"This is the first stanza. Impressions?"

"Five, eight, nine, nine," spoke Jerry, a real talent. "What is that?"

"Well, it has its own sequence."

"Sure. And I like the theme, or rather, the idea," spoke Jennifer, a brain who took the course because of her thirst for learning. "Who was she?" she asked.

"Later," Vince gave them, as the class laughed and loosened up.

"So, we find our own structure based on what we must say about love, desire, feelings, and all that?" asked a black student.

"All that. By now each of you knows whether this is just part of your academic process to get a degree, or to follow a life calling. You'll always be able to use this as you go along. Few writers do just that; write, I mean. And especially poets. Rappers of old did it, but now it's about the business. I love words and must write, and teaching allows me to do that. But I never wanted to sit around and just be cool, or esoteric. It's all about a feeling for me, a mental 'wiggle' I call it," Vince espouses.

"So, we find our voice by way of the method?" Jerry asked.

"Maybe. It could be the other way around. Lyric, narrative, dramatic, it's all there, your choice," he told them.

"So, cadence is what?" Jennifer asked.

"It depends. Certain schools want the classical interpretations. What's said is secondary. I never could follow that, and probably won't. My poems come full blown, and it's my job to record them. Like I said before it's the music, standard or otherwise. Each writer should follow their happy place, as it were. We'll look at the second stanza tomorrow and see what comes next. Some of you may be surprised. Have a great day."

The twelve students shuffle about, stop to talk with one another, and move on to the next class. Vince decides to make that call.

*

Dr. Bethany Richards returned to her office about 1:30p.m. She waved to her assistant to hold everything for a few moments as she entered and closed the door to her sanctuary. It had been a full day already and she needed to sit quietly, alone. She fixed a cup of tea and sat in the chair facing the desk. She looked out the window, transfixed on her thoughts. After tea, and twenty minutes later she came out to get caught up on the rest of her schedule. Melissa had laid everything out for her on the left side of her desk, and Beth thanked her, picked up the files and returned to her desk, sitting on the other side now. After answering some billing questions from utilization review, and dictating notes on today's results, she checked her messages. At number 10 of 25 was a message from Vince: "Didn't know you were a doctor? When will you have time for coffee?"

She called him back, but got the voice mail prompt, and responded, "Didn't know you were a professor, when is your last class?"

They finally connect about four o'clock and talk for an hour.

"Bethany Richards, this is Vincent Edwards, we met at the party Saturday night," he starts when she answers.

"Vincent how are you?" she says.

"Good, good. Just thought I would give you a call. How are you?"

"I'm good, things are busy, but good. Thanks for calling."

"Sure, thanks for spending time with me. I had a nice time at the party; it was good," he says.

"It was good. They are such good people. Susie and I go back to high school," she tells him.

"Great. Mark was cordial. Did they invite me to meet you?" he asks her.

"I don't know, could be that fate thing?" she says to him.

"Well, it was great, being new to the area and all. I needed to loosen up, and feel more a part of the community," Vince says to her.

"It's a great town. Lots of art minded people. Nice, open, comfortable," she mentions.

"So, what kind of doctor are you; I couldn't find out much?" he questions.

"That's okay, I'm kind of low key. Research. Addiction Studies."

"Wow. How did you get into that?" he asks.

"Curiosity. Intellectual, then practical. I'm in recovery," she reveals to him.

"Wow. May I ask...?"

"Sure, I'm open. But not much there. Do you know much about addiction?" she asks.

"Not much. I drink a little, like at the party, and I've tried stuff, but pretty much straight. I've read a little, and I had a few friends go off the deep end back in Atlanta. You'll have to school me."

"Sure. Poet?"

"Yeah, pretty simple. Born to write."

"That's easy enough."

"Mostly. It's a curious field these days for a guy like me. I don't do readings much or belong to a book club. I just basically write. I published a book a few years ago, and I teach. Simple. Of course, I'll get you one of my books, or you can fund my retirement by buying one."

"Sure. I can do poetry. So, I liked sleeping pills and pot. Just enough nod, and just enough dream state. It became every day for a little over a year and I sought treatment. I've been clean for nine months, and I go to 12 step meetings. My doctoral thesis was about 'The Dream State: How Integration Made Us Separate. The Pain of Getting to Know One Another.' The pills got me through that."

"Man, that's a lot to take in all at once. You're pretty deep sister."

"I'll take that as a compliment."

"That's the way it's meant. I tried a little pot, some coke, you know, but it wasn't for me. I didn't even finish the drink I had at the party. Just not my deal."

"So, I'm thirty-two, and have been around the block. You're about thirty, and went home early?"

"That's an interesting way to put it. Thirty-three next month actually."

"Oh, got me by a month."

"Okay, so, lunch, dinner or something soon?" he asks her.

"Yes. Let's talk again and see what we can come up with?" she replies.

"I'm in. Take care."

"You too. Thanks for calling. Good bye."

"Okay, take care. Good bye."

***

Tucker was eighty miles east of Atlanta, Georgia. It was a quiet manufacturing town of about 18,000 residents back in 1986. There was a kitchen and bath cabinet maker that employed about 20 people, the automobile company that ran two shifts, and employed 1,500, and their parts division that kept another 400 working. There were about ten related businesses that kept 100 or so locals going, and the local government agency at full staff had a hundred workers and administrative personnel. The college employed about 150, and the hospital usually ran about 180. Unemployment was low at 6.5 percent due to the many shops, farms, and eateries scattered over the 25-square mile area. The racial mix was 70 percent white, and 30 percent non-white. By most indicators, the standard of living was adequate, and the city government had been run by good, decent citizens for a long time, though there were some issues back in 1969 that got the federal government's attention and caused heartache for the town's leaders and citizens. That passed, and the town is now known as a good place to live, raise a family, and move forward.

Mark Davis and Susie Little's families lived a street over from each other, and Mark played with Susie's brother Arnold, and the other boys from sun up to sun down, running all over the woods, and playgrounds near the youth clubs. Mark was a good kid, smart and a bit hyperactive. His mouth would get him in trouble sometimes when he spent too much time with boys who were not his equal, whether at sports or academics. He averaged about three good fights a year between the ages of ten and 16, then smoothed out when he took a liking to Susie. They would go out, and do things, and it was good to see them at the movies, the mall, or just hanging out with other kids.

Susie was sweet, and gentle, but had a determination to do well. She took to her chores, school work, and activities with the same zeal, and would fight for what she thought was right. She wanted to be a business woman, and learned good work habits early, listening and watching what her parents did to make a success of their food enterprise franchise. Susie would work a few hours a week, enjoyed meeting people, and the paychecks she received every other week. She was the lead clerk by the time she went off to college.

Bobby Maddox lived down the street from Mark and fought with him more than anyone else. It would usually be ruled a tie as they didn't want to hurt the other one, it was more a test of strength and quickness.

Mark was the better puncher, and Bobby had more endurance. They stayed friends, even after Bobby moved away for many years.

CHAPTER 2

Opening day for the shop they were up at four a.m. They showered together, giggled a lot, and hurried about the apartment getting dressed and ready, trying not to make too much noise and disturb the neighbors. They settled down enough to have a breakfast of grits and eggs and drank milk and coffee. Before heading out the door they embraced, and said a prayer, asking for guidance and goodness. They made the short drive down Moreland, cut through to Montgomery, and saw the sign as they turned onto Hardee, "Coffee and Cakes." They smiled to each other.

Susie had the honor of inserting the key and opening the front door. They stepped in, held hands, and just looked around at what they had accomplished thus far. It was neat and clean, with second hand wooden tables and chairs. The air smelled of the baked goods and coffee beans put into stock yesterday. The tile floor sparkled, and the windows were free of smudges. Even though they both would handle all necessary job functions, Susie ran the register and took orders, and Mark brought out the slices of cake on paper plates. Customers could pour coffee and get a fork and napkins from the service counter. It was a nice, smooth operation, and the first day they had 40 customers.

"Wow, what a day," Mark commented as they cleaned up crumbs and stains from the busy day.

"Wow, can you believe it!" Susie echoed. "This was great! All the people! And our parents coming in; what a treat!"

"I almost lost it when mom and dad came in," Mark says. "And to see the smile on your dad's face was unbelievable."

"That was precious. And mom's hug was great. We are very fortunate," Susie says to him. Yes, we are, and I love you very much," Mark says, taking her left hand.

"Likewise, to you," she says, and gives him a peck on the cheek.

They lock up, and head home, still all smiles.

Beth did not know where she was, or who the man sitting next to her was either. It was a rather long and fully padded sofa, and she felt a tightness in her neck, on the right side, as she looked around the room counting three other people, one on the floor, and two motionless in chairs not made for sleeping. She felt drowsy, and her mouth was dry from the pot and pills she ingested last night. She wanted to stand and go pee, but wasn't sure of her bearing, nor did she know where the restroom was. Best she could tell it was a nice house, but whose was it? She didn't feel afraid, just confused as to where she was, how she got there, and what happened? Slowly the memory wheel started turning: the ceremony, food and drinks with co-workers, introduction to Ben, ride to Sarah's house, beer, a sleeping pill, the joints being passed around. She couldn't recall much else. She was fully clothed, and not too rumbled, and she knew she had to go to the bathroom soon. She forced herself up, stood in place a moment, and placed one foot in front of the other, across the room to a hallway to her right. The bathroom was there, and a woman was passed out on the floor such that she had to step over and past her to take a seat. She pushed the woman back from the toilet, wiped the seat off with a paper towel from a rack nearby, and took care of her business. The woman groaned a bit, and changed her position back to where it was, her head landing on Beth's left foot. Beth shook it off, pulled her pants up, flushed, and got out of there quickly, a bit panicked now.

When she went out to the room, she recognized the man and woman in the chairs, Joe, and Mindy Ferguson, but the person on the floor was a mystery, as well as the man on the sofa. Being a doctor, though not a medical doctor, she checked to see if everyone was breathing, they were, and she started her exit plan. "Where the hell am I, and how did I get here?"

*

Vince had decided to take the job at the community college in Brewton. His first book of poetry had been published, and the administration was quite pleased that he accepted their offer to teach there. He would develop a standard curriculum around the elements of writing poetry. He had reservations at first, but they assured him there was room for traditional, and non- traditional methodology to be taught. They wanted him, and what he had accomplished as a writer.

*

The Institute for Addiction Studies was well funded by private donations, and Beth was grateful to be given the opportunity to work there and collect stories from people who were addicted. She needed one more story to meet a publishing deadline and chose one at random from a stack of twenty-seven on her desk. It was from someone who was in prison, or who had been to prison, she wasn't sure. She was reading it for the third time, and was still not sure about its process, but she knew she wanted it to be a part of the study.

CHAPTER 3

I was on the Train to Tucker, breathing heavily, sweating. I had killed Jake Austin, or so I thought, and Leroy Fleming, his assistant, the felon, spotted me in the second car, sitting by the pregnant woman. I knew he would want to talk, he was not like his brother Larry, the trained assassin. I was tired, and my mission had failed. All I knew was that I was supposed to get rid of Jake, and I would receive the rest of the money to disappear. They didn't tell me about Leroy, or I would have told them no, that we had history. Jake and Leroy had become like brothers. This was not good. When the train stopped, he motioned me to get off and go with him. I stood and followed behind him.

Marie rushed to the hospital and smiled when Jake could wave to her. He had been out of surgery for over six hours, and all signs were positive for a full recovery. His liver was damaged, and he may lose sight in his right eye, but otherwise he was okay. The nurse gave her a clinical update, and said he needed to rest now. Marie went over to hug him, kissed him on the mouth, and settled into a chair pulled up close to the bed, tripping over the robot monitor recording vital signs every ten minutes. She was worried about safety until Leroy called an hour later. She stepped out of the room and went to a waiting area just past the nurses' station.

"Hello."

"Hey Marie, Leroy. How are you?" he asked.

"Well, afraid, but somewhat relieved," she told him.

"Celia should be there shortly," he told her.

"Good. About the attack?" she asked.

"Not random, and I know why it happened. I'll tell you more later," he gave her.

"Thanks Leroy. You're the best."

"Okay. I'll be there in about an hour."

*

Eight months ago, Jake had decided to return to the chip manufacturing business. He had bought property outside of the perimeter, and built a 'fab' that was state of the art. There were sixteen robots that ran the place, and four humans that programmed the systems. Their latest chip had surpassed the internet of things and returned to individual process. One morning Robot Fourteen inadvertently split a disk that went into a power plant delivery system and improved efficiency 16%. The resulting sales had climbed to 2.5 billion dollars in three months, and the SR14 Chip had become an industry standard for power grid distribution.

*

Thomas Jeter, head of BYA Industries, wanted to buy Jake out, and Jake had refused an offer of 18 billion. Jeter was not to be denied and had set other plans in motion that could disrupt the $450 billion-dollar silicon chip industry. Jake was well respected in the chip world, and his return to differentiated transistors was nothing less than genius. The attempt on his life was unprovoked, though the rumor mills were circulating that someone close to Jeter had been put out of business when Jake closed Triple Line Systems back in 2013, after the sale of WES, to Henson Technologies, the company his mentor Wallace Henson had built to prominence. They did not want to see Jake prosper, again, nor live, for that matter.

*

Jake could sense his father speaking to him, "don't give up." It seemed odd because Jake was not a quitter. He knew he was injured, but never felt the death angel coming for him. He could still see Marie and the kids at church, on vacation, and even at Ashley's high school graduation. He felt the pain in his side and thought that to be from the way he crossed his right leg up high over the left knee. He didn't know he had been shot yet as he was in a coma of sorts, his brain shutting down to keep the fighter in him from going after the men who had come to his car. His head hurt, and the vision in his right eye was blurry, fortunately it was a small caliber weapon. "You can't have my car!" he told the lighter skinned boy, the one with the gun. He looked at the other boy, darker in skin tone, who fumbled with a large knife, that he dropped as he panicked, seeing all the blood. He could feel his hands slip from the steering wheel, and his head wobble on his neck. He felt weak, and alone, before praying, "help me father, help me." He could vaguely hear the sirens as the day darkened, and he sensed the blood where his hand pushed against his belly, pushing back what would not stop. He remembered the woman saying, "you're going to be okay."

"Bobby, why did you try to take my man out?" Leroy asked him.

"Jeter," was all he said.

"Is there going to be another problem?" he asked me.

"Maybe. He wants the business; he's obsessed, and jealous."

"Where does this leave you?" Leroy asked him.

"You'll never hear from me again. I just needed some cash. This was stupid," he said to Leroy.

"What's next?" Leroy asked him, becoming somewhat angry.

"There was an appeal. Be sure and review all patents granted to WES and sold to Henson Technologies. That's where Jake comes in. You may want to consult with Thomas Robinson."

"I thought all that was settled?"

"I guess you really don't know why I was disbarred from practicing law?"

"No, I don't."

"Do you remember Sally Penfield, the lawyer who handled the sale?"

"That was before my time with Jake."

"Anyway, when you talk to Robinson, ask him about his former attorney, Randall Brewer, and his cousin, Horace Lincoln, patent attorney. It will explain why they came after Jake this way. Of course, I don't need to tell you to be careful."

"Anything else?"

"I could use some traveling money."

CHAPTER 4

Dr. Howard Elam rechecked Jake's eye charts and verified that he was at 65 percent sight restoration. This, and the normal liver enzyme test results he was given yesterday were good news. Two months had passed, and no one wanted Jake back at work yet. Leroy had been installed as interim CEO and was fully in charge of all facets of the business. Marie was spending more time at the office and would take feeds from him home for Jake to review. The only concern was that Jake's recall was faulty, and he would have periods of dis-association. He was receiving cognitive therapy twice a week, and the doctors felt he was at least stable, and had a base line of functioning that could facilitate a good quality of life if aggressive monitoring were maintained. Still, he was not well, and had not expressed a desire to return to the office.

*

The altered chip design was no mistake. Robot Fourteen had learned how to upgrade the programs presented by Hunter Davis, the chief engineer. Hunter had thought it was a placement problem when the wafers were installed into the hardware. Even though his design was making the company a lot of money as the key of choice for so many devices, Hunter could no longer take credit for the success, privately. He knew 'Fourteen' had autonomously changed some code. With Jake sidelined, he needed to talk to Leroy and Marie.

*

"Jeter here," Thomas Jeter answered the phone.
    "Hey Thomas, It's Bobby."
    "Why are you calling me? We have no more business."
    "I think we do. Jake Austin's assistant, Leroy Fleming, is running the company now."

"That doesn't affect me."

"It will, in time."

"Bobby, never call me again. Why did you use those punks to do men's work? Get some help for yourself. Your judgement is off. You're still in bad shape."

Jeter ended the call, cleared his call log, and assembled his legal team.

CHAPTER 5

Jake stood outside about this time yesterday admiring the diamond like sparkle of the blown green leaves, fluttering up and down, back, and forth, quickly, slowly, getting back in place, awaiting the wind speed change to sparkle again from the brightness of the overhead sunlight.

The trees were mostly white oak, the ones near the top of the hill, and the ones set in the woods were mostly maple. Of course, there were the ever-present pines, tall, spacious, and flowing at the top, this being north Georgia and all.

He and Marie loved this community, with its country feel, due to the quietness of the village of mostly retired folks. The lush, mid-spring air was clean and wholesome, as every fifth house either had a resident gardener, or had been landscaped by knowledgeable workers. There were a lot of green, variegated plants, but enough color from the perennials to make the 64 houses enclave a magical place.

Marie had stood at the den window both days watching him. He seemed peaceful enough, and the rehabilitation staff had told her he would be discharged from outpatient care next week. She agreed that he had made tremendous progress the past month, and they both were adjusting to this new normal.

She found herself dealing with a deep anger towards the teenagers who did this to her beloved husband. Though she believed in forgiveness, she had expressed to their family attorney to make sure they received the fullest punishment possible. Jake could videotape his version of the assault, and though it was brief, when added to several witness accounts, would help the prosecution's presentation against the teens. Marie was glad about that and made plans to celebrate Jake's forty ninth birthday next week.

*

Bobby Maddox had been out of prison a year and a half when he sought treatment. His alcohol use was out of control again, and he couldn't stop on his own. Mark and Susie had put him up for a few weeks but asked him to leave when he stole some money from the café. Dexter Jeter had checked into the same rehab and remembered Bobby from the appeal his company lost, or rather had overturned by a judge partial to the interests of Triple Line Systems. They had not talked of those matters, but when Dexter's alcoholic fog cleared after two weeks he remembered Bobby and had words with him at dinner one evening.

"You seem familiar to me?" Dexter asked on approach.

"Have a seat," Bobby offered. "How was detox?"

"Bobby, Bobby Maddox, attorney, or should I say ex-attorney?"

"I guess you have cleared. They didn't think you were going to make it. Blood and vomit, bad stuff," Bobby said to him.

"Look, you owe me, and you will pay up!" Dexter said to him.

"Mistakes were made all around," Bobby offered.

"Mistakes my ass, you cost me a fortune!"

"It was not all my fault."

"Well forget it. You just messed up."

Dexter threw his food tray at Bobby, a direct hit to the forehead. Staff helped Bobby clean up, and Dexter was taken to seclusion.

*

Bobby hadn't eaten in two days when he checked into the rehabilitation center. He was to the point of eating out of trash bins when he reminded himself, "I am an attorney, after all." The incident with Dexter solidified his desire to recover, and he accepted the fact that low as he was he was not going to give up. He had given up on himself before, but now was the time to get better. His five-year slide to obscurity was over.

*

"I like men with secrets," Jake Austin shared with Leroy, "and you have to live a great life to have them. Some men are fortunate that way."

"Who are you talking about Jake?" Leroy asked him.

"You actually, and how you have handled things since I've been away. It's been a real comfort; our whole relationship, I mean, the way it has developed," Jake gives him.

"It is pretty cool. So, what's next?" Leroy asks.

"Robot Fourteen."

"Robot Fourteen. Jake, that's a problem. It is now writing simultaneous code to correct Mr. Hunter's versions. They even work better," Leroy informs him. "Plus, it wants me to continue to run the company. It says you will die soon."

"That's drastic, from code to fortune telling. Should we just dismantle it?"

"We can't. It developed a scenario to infect every sensor we've produced in the last seven months if we do that," Leroy tells him.

"What's our move?"

"A guy I know, Robert Maddox."

"Tech wiz?"

"No, dope fiend."

CHAPTER 6

"Okay, second stanza," Vincent announced to the class.

   Life with you will be my task,
   Ups and downs, sickness, and health,
   I'll see if I can destroy my mask,
   And gain a life of happy wealth.

"You were how old when you wrote this?" a female student asked.

"Your age maybe, nineteen," Vincent offered.

"Was there really a girlfriend?" Garner asked.

"No. I was dreaming."

The students laugh and look around at each other.

"How about the measures?" Jennifer followed.

"Didn't matter, I was saying what needed to be expressed."

"So, you really don't follow the rules?" Jerry commented. "But you do have a structure."

"Precisely. And it must work, or I'm fooling myself. To be called a poet one should have a command of their thoughts, then the language. Not the other way around. Thought leads to language. Precision comes in telling the story, the who, what, when, where, and how."

"Journalism?"

"Maybe. It's what kind of story do you want to tell. And really, the poet never knows."

"Old brain, new brain stuff?" Garner asks.

"Well yes. Feeling before thought, otherwise, you're just reporting. The poet creates with the language because the feeling has no meaning. That's why like Garner suggests, the old brain is driving the train. A poet can exist without language, but a reporter can't. The story finds the poet, but the reporter has to find the story!"

CHAPTER 7

Beth found herself thinking of Vince more and more. She wanted to stop it, but something was happening that was nice, yet scary. She was enjoying 'clean and sober,' and the job was great. She would have to visit her parents soon and was trying to figure out if Thanksgiving was the best time, but that was three months away. She drifted off to sleep, and had a weird dream:

We knew the storm was coming. It was about two in the afternoon, and I was near the inlet, shorts, and t-shirt on, looking. Tide was high, and the waves were flush and demanding. I was smiling, "Maybe not." Irene was further down the beach calling for me to come back. I ignored her, present with the air, the breeze, the clouds, sunlight. After a few moments, I turned, waved to her, and screamed, "It's not coming!"

We had left our second home in South Carolina the day before Hurricane Hugo hit in 1989, when the water was turbulent, and the wind was telling; there was no doubt then that the storm was coming, as it did. We lost a condo, and a car, but learned to trust the wind, and the forecasters, mostly.

She was ageing nicely, I thought. Sure, gravity and wear had taken something away from her beauty, but we got together when we were in our early forties, lush, full, and vigorous. I was working long hours, and she was flying about presenting her art works to clients. She had just come back from Florence when we met, and I had not dated in several months. My best friend, Charles Lawson, had tried to set me up a couple of times, but I had no interest. The pain of divorce was still fresh, and I was busy running from project to project, saving money, preparing for whatever was next. I was surprised though, when I stopped long enough to realize that I had not been on a vacation in two years, and that all the credit cards were paid in full. I met her at a coffee shop and didn't shave on purpose that morning. I was tired and needed a break.

"Hello," she said, coming to the assigned meeting table at the side window of Harry's Deli. "I'm Irene."

Standing, and offering a hand, I say, "Hi, I'm Tony. Please, sit down."

She gives a faint smile and looks directly at me before placing her small purse on the table and saying, "Charles said you may be a little rough around the edges, you look tired."

"I am actually," I offer, feeling that this was too personal already.

"There are remedies for that. I'm just back from Europe, and it was great. Ten days of art, low light, and good wine. I'm an artist," she boasts.

"I've heard, and I've seen your work. Pretty good."

"Is that all, 'pretty good!' she mocks. "I'll get you back!"

We both laugh, I more so than her as I hadn't felt this loose around a woman in a long time.

"I mean, you know," I try to explain.

"And I hear you run a 'good' office!"

"Okay. Okay. Coffee?"

"No, I came here for sex."

"I thought you said artist, not comedian," I comment, and we laugh some more.

"Should we start over?" she asks.

"No, let's go for a walk, and get the coffee to go? I'll pay for it."

"A Southern Gentleman; this is good."

"You don't stop do you?"

"Not if it's good clean fun."

We went on like that for weeks, meeting, eating, just enjoying being together. The conversations were all over the place as we both seemed to have needed this kind of pleasure, with no pressure, no pretense; just the excitement of early love, which neither expected. She had never married, and I needed the hope produced by our dating. Having a friend again was good.

*

I left the office about seven, Chris and Raymond had left about five; it had been a good day. We made seven-hundred and fifty dollars, and there would be orders to ship in the morning. Our greeting cards were catching on, and operating costs were stabilizing. Chris had changed the advertising pitch and some investments Raymond made with some of the profit from last year were paying a small return. All signs pointed northward, and our little adventure was becoming a business. They generally worked six, seven hours a day now, but I still stayed around thinking about the day, and what we would need to do tomorrow. Ten hours a day had become my normal output, and that did not change until I met Irene. My first marriage ended when we started the business, and I didn't want a repeat performance.

*

Irene had two upcoming trips, one to Taos, and the other to Phoenix. She asked if I would join her and use the time as my vacation. It sounded great, but I wasn't sure if I was ready to not work for two weeks. Chris and Ray sided with her, and I agreed. We would fly out Saturday and return the following Friday. She had six galleries to visit, three in each city, and she said I could act as her assistant.

"I thought I was supposed to be off work?" I protested, as we loaded her portfolio luggage into the car.

"I'm not paying you. You are an intern," she said.

"What am I training for?" I asked.

"To be my rock," she said.

"Oh, so soon?"

"Remember, training, not yet certified!"

We laughed, got the car loaded, and headed for the airport. It was beginning to rain, and I hoped our flight would not be delayed, impatient sort that I am.

As we got closer to Hartsfield we could see the smoke rising over near the controller's tower. Suddenly, the wail of fire engines came upon us and we, like the others on this stretch of I-285, slowed, and pulled over to let them pass trouble free; four in all. "This is not good," Irene commented.

"No, something bad has happened. What should we do?" I ask.

"Let's continue and see if we can contact Travel Flight."

"Okay. Let me call them." I call and get a recorded message:

"If you have a scheduled flight with Travel Flight this morning it has been postponed. This message will update every thirty minutes until an all clear is achieved. Thank you."

"Wow! What do you think has happened?" Irene asked at the end of the message.

"I don't know, but the smoke trail has widened and become darker. Let me check The News Channel's app and see if they know anything?" I say to her.

I pulled over and put the car in park, as other cars did the same. I press the app button to a news flash: "Fire in hanger at Hartsfield, no fatalities reported, several people injured with burns and concussion type events. The fire was contained to a storage area, but the airport has suspended all departures and arrivals until further notice. Could be the rest of the morning until damage is assessed, and all are accounted for."

"Well that's good news, I mean considering what we usually hear these days," Irene offers.

"True. I guess we'll head back?"

"To where?"

"Your place I guess?"

"Yeah, that's fine," she responds.

"Somewhere else?"

"No, I'm just thinking."

"Terrorist?"

"Yeah, the world is so crazy now. It can't be just a plain old accident anymore; of course, it may be, but the news."

"I know, it is crazy. I guess we could stop off at Jaimoe's for breakfast?"

"Good idea."

*

Jaimoe's was in a rough area of town, old city. There were small, abandoned shop buildings and clap board houses from the 1920s that were pieced together to form a good community. The look and feel were due to architectural changes that moved everyone into the 20th century. People worked, and took care of what they had, large families staked their claim to a small plot of land, and neighbors knew each other. The neighborhoods were mature, and Pecan and Peach trees still produced, Muscadine grape droppings stained sidewalks, and Fig trees still put out large, full fruit by the bushel that was shared, and traded family to family for resources they had. It was a cityscape from a bygone era as blacks came up from the country and built new lives on the east side of the bustling town known as Atlanta.

So much changed around 1980 as older blacks died off, and so much was left behind. There were failed attempts by young people to save the area, but family members who had been deeded properties didn't keep them up, and so many houses were abandoned. It took a few years, and a depressed financial market to make it attractive for investors to buy in and start the trend towards craftsman style housing on double lots.

Irene was a part of this wave of professionals who bought in at the right time, not idealistic in the usual sense, but hopeful, and experienced enough to know how difficult it can be for change to force certain elements away from the only life they've known. Prison, drugs, and illness had taken its toll, and many former residents had been defeated and moved on. A stronger, more mature populace would have to care for them now, somewhere else, as these younger folks had other concerns. It was the new greening of the area starting in 1989.

*

When we arrived, about nine-thirty, most of the court people had come, figured out an angle for the day, and were near, or already at their duty stations. The left overs were the business players, and the semi-retired of various persuasions. Jaimoe Heard had been feeding them for the past eighteen years, and most came by at least once a week. These were Atlanta folks, sophisticated, urbane, and full of success. They had not marched so much but were the direct beneficiaries of the struggle. They went to schools out of state, and came back, ready to set up homes in the newer communities. They got the good jobs, and were making a difference by the steady, everyday work ethic their parents had shown them. They didn't question much, and the 'wait and see' approach had served most well. They were in their fifties now, and some had gone to high school with Jaimoe, and still sang his praises for carrying the football team to a winning season back in 1979. Everybody remembered his thirty-yard touchdown run to beat Brown 21 to 18 that gave them the 5-4-1 record. It inspired others to step up in basketball, baseball, and in the classroom. He did not go on to college but worked with his grandfather cutting grass for six years, saved some cash, then he developed a plan to open a restaurant. Friends invested money and time, and it opened to great fanfare and promise the spring of 1998. Everybody came to get a meal with Jaimoe and support his dream.

The building was an Ice Cream Plant built in 1924. It was all brick, one tone, and quite functional for its intended purpose. It was easy to heat in winter, and cool in the summer, and the company was there until 1990. There were code renovations over the years until they closed it and moved the operation to Newnan. Only six out of 20 employees could transfer to that area 60 miles away. The building had been vacant until Jaimoe bought it. He and his partners could maintain the period look, but updated lighting, walls, and wiring to accommodate the styles of the modern push to openness, and structural visibility inside. It could seat thirty-five patrons comfortably. During peak business hours, there could be a short wait to get seated. We were able to walk right in and grab a booth. It didn't take the hostess long to come over and greet us, she and Irene knew each other. Irene had been a regular customer the past five years.

"Hey darling," spoke Lynn as she got closer to us, waving a hand of acknowledgement.

"Hey sweetie, how are you?" Irene returned.

"I'm fine, good to see you all. And who is this?" she questioned.

"He's a friend, Anthony."

"A friend, or your friend?"

We looked at each other as Irene weighed her response.

"My friend," she answers.

"Good looking; I would claim him too. Hi Tony, I'm Lynn. Glad to have you here."

"Thank you. I've been here before, several times. Great place."

"I guess I've missed you. I have been away some the past two years," she offers, and looks over to Irene.

"Oh," Irene stumbles. "Just water, coffee later, maybe."

"I'll have a coffee now," Tony says to her.

"Are y'all ready to order?" Lynn asks rather curtly.

"Sure, sure," Irene responds. "I'll have a cheese, egg, and tomato omelet."

"Same here," Tony says.

"Okay, Liz will bring them right out," Lynn says, turning and walking away quickly.

"Boy, that got uncomfortable in a hurry?" Tony states to Irene.
"Rehab a couple of times. I still don't think she's clean."
"Okay. Memo to file."

*

We received a text message about noon that the explosion was ruled an accident, too much combustible material and a heat source coming together at the right time in a confined area. Two workers sustained injuries and were hospitalized. Damage was still being assessed, and the airport had resumed operations. Flights had been delayed six hours. Our new departure time was two-thirty, so we left Jaimoe's and returned to the airport. We parked, checked in, and took up a position to 'people watch' one gate over from our assigned departure gate. It was for incoming flights from Rome.

When we arrived at the gate two airline employees were finishing duties associated with a departing flight; it was going to Nevada. The Rome flight was scheduled to arrive at one-forty-five, so we had time to relax, watch, and further our relationship inquiries until our departure flight to Albuquerque, New Mexico. We were six weeks into this, and it certainly was feeling like a big deal. She acted as though we had known each other forever. I was scared most of the time, even though things had gone along rather nicely. I had met her brother Jeff, and his wife, Dana, so that was cool, but I still wasn't sure if I wanted to be a 'couple' yet, even though we were acting that way. I guess the main thing was I didn't have any control over events. She usually had the plans, and I was just going along, which was nice in a lot of ways. I was thinking that maybe I should just enjoy the ride, and take a dual vacation, one from work, and the other away from my brain. It didn't seem to be working well, however. Then I heard a loud voice coming from the wall nearest the last newspaper shop.

"Anthony Crawford, hey, how did you get in here?" spoke Lanny, a friend from college whom I had not seen in ten years. "What's going on man?"

He walks, no, almost trots over to where we were sitting, all smiles, and 240 pounds of friendliness.

"Hey, Anthony Crawford, best friend ever," he boasts as he looks over to Irene, and steps to me, arms wide open, waiting for a hug. I stand and brace my 190-pound frame for the ensuing jolt. He bounces into me, leans his head back, and says, "Man I am glad I ran into you!" I try to loosen his grip, but he holds on for a few seconds, then finally reaches over to shake Irene's hand, and introduce himself to her. "I'm Lanny, I owe this man everything." She stands, and he gives her a hug; not as tight. "I'm Irene," she says to him.

"Look, my wife Corliss should be coming out of the news shop in a minute, I want you to meet her," he goes on. He blows out a breath, and motions for all to sit down. He grabs his chest.

"Whew, this is exciting. Anthony Crawford. My man."

Corliss walks out of the newsstand and is surprised to see us; it was Lynn, at least that's the name Irene and I knew her by. Lanny motioned for her to come over, but she turned and went towards the escalator. Lanny, shocked, went after her, "Corliss, what's the matter?" he shouted, looked back at us, and kept going after her.

*

Phoenix was first. Irene received a text message about four-thirty from Ira and Jean Maddison that they could not meet us at the airport, but please come by for dinner at eight. Their home address was listed. We landed safely, gathered our belongings, picked out a rental car, and headed South down 10 for our hotel near Gilbert. Jean called about seven local time.

"Irene, Jean. How's it going?"

"Great. Good flight, no worries."

"Good, sorry we could not meet you as planned. Where are you?"
"Just checking in to the hotel."
"Great. We're about 20 minutes away. Did you get the map?"
"We did. We'll get settled and see you about eight or so."
"That's good. Okay. See you then."

*

"Getting back to your friend," Irene asked as we unpacked and placed items around the rooms, then interjected, "I usually like the left side of the bed, does that work for you?"

"Sure," I said, and moved my slacks, shirts, and socks to the other side of the bed.

"So, Lanny, what was that about?"

"I'm not sure. Curious though that he said Lynn was his wife. I helped Lanny out of a bad spot one time. He was about to get jumped and robbed, and I stepped in."

"What did you do?"

"I knew the guys, and spoke up that Lanny was my friend, and if they were going to jump him they were going to have a problem with me."

"They backed off, just like that?"

"No. I had to fight one of them, Avery Thompson, who's in prison now. It wasn't too bad, and Lanny was appreciative."

"You're a hero."

"Yeah. I'm just glad it was over quickly. Now tell me what you know about 'Corliss,'" I ask her.

"That was strange! I just know that she's been a waitress there at Jaimoe's, and there would be talk that she was a problem child. Tips missing, drama, she would go off to rehab, and Jai would just let her come back. She was a good hostess, and waitress for that matter, but obviously, she had some issues."

"Well, I just hope Lanny's okay, and her for that matter. He's my age of course, but she looked much older. Forty-five maybe?"

"Maybe. Could be the hard living that's aged her."

*

The Maddison's lived in a nice community on the east side of Gilbert. More commercial development was taking over as a five-acre lot was being cleared for a senior living residence to open next summer. It would be a mile and a half away so not much disruption to the quiet setting of their home, though you could hear the rumble of heavy equipment during business hours. They were usually up in Phoenix four days a week at their gallery, and still travelled a good bit to art shows and the like, so they weren't too affected by the changes. Their moderately priced ranch style home was well insulated, and the high wall around the subdivision provided a certain amount of noise reduction for the area. A hay field six blocks away from their house was mowed over last year, and the land was sold to a developer whose mixed-use development is about sixty percent complete. The area is changing, but it was still very nice, and comfortable.

"I think this is it," Irene stated in synch with the voice of the GPS system, "Take right turn in 100 feet," it said. "Your destination will be on the left."

The street was well lit, and the house was inviting from the outside. "Well, this is it," Irene said, surveying this and several other houses nearby, "1427. Nice," she said, more to herself than to me.

"I like the rock garden with cactus. I guess that's the way they do it out here," I comment.

"We're in the desert you know," she mentions.

"I wasn't trying to be funny," I say to her. "Well, it just sounded like you were making a judgement."

"Well, I am from back east, grass, bushes, kudzu, you know."

"You've got to get out more."

As they parked two figures appeared at the front door of the home, waving, and smiling.

*

Lanny could see Corliss, but he wasn't sure he was going to catch up with her before she got into the cab. She had done things like this before in the three years they had been together, but this was a little different. "What, or who had she seen; and why the urgency to flee?" It was a curious puzzle, and this time Lanny had to let her go.

*

Bethany woke up about seven and tried to make sense of the dream. None of it fit with what she had been thinking before drifting off to sleep. Issues from the past perhaps? At any rate, she smiled again as she thought of spending more time with Vince, 'The Poet!'

CHAPTER 8

Jake and Marie were having a simple meal of turkey and kale when the text came through; It was from Fourteen. "Sorry I had to change the codes and put in the protections. You will thank me later."

Jake showed it to Marie after reading it. "How can a machine do this?" Marie asked, rather innocently.

"I'm not sure if it's just the machine, or someone behind the machine. It is rather frightening. I'm anxious to meet Leroy's friend to see what he has to say."

"You don't think it's Leroy, do you?" she asked him.

"I don't think so," Jake fudged his answer as he had to suspect everyone. "This is about a lot of money and power, and the courts were due a ruling on states' rights to control energy production. It was this whole move towards nationalization that is ultimately at stake, and somehow technology has controlled the debate. The people abdicated power to affect change themselves, and now the algorithms have taken over. Fourteen is only a beginning."

"How so?" she asks.

"Take for instance the health care industry, the insurers I mean. If they promote health enough people will opt out. What academia has not done is train more doctors in alternative health. Health care is a right, but people have to own the new choices."

"You mean the right choices?"

"Yes. Just like me now, healthy, great insurance, survived a vicious attack, and the insurers will pay."

"I see where you're going, one system to take care of us all."

"Gets back to ethical behaviors!"

"Okay, so, you do trust Leroy, right?"

"Absolutely."

*

Beth and Vince were getting cozy, and they spent a Sunday together just sitting around at her place, eating, talking, reading on their devices, and generally being together. Beth had celebrated a year clean at her meeting last week, and Vince attended.

"That was kind of cool last week, your meeting I mean," he offered up.

"Yeah, it's important. I'm glad you came."

"Is there much confusion about your work and what you have to do for yourself?" he asked.

"Sometimes. My recovery comes first though, period, then the work."

"How about what you're working on now, and that dream you told me about?"

"That was kind of deep. I'm still not sure what that was about."

"Would that be the therapy stuff?"

"I suppose. I hadn't thought much about it. If it's something I should look at, as they say, I will."

"May I read you my latest poem?"

"I'd love to hear it."

Vince stands, motions as if to an audience and begins:
Morning cool, summer late, I sit and watch my phone,
to organize, and breathe new air,
beneath this tree of life.

"I guess, whatever it is you have, you have it; beautiful!"

*

The Thomas H. Jeter Building was set just outside the perimeter highway. The area was designated Class-A Structures, but his stood out from the newer, hybrid-towers built since 2002 because his two-story was made of red clay bricks from the 1930s, and due to the dark, rough surface of the second story brick it looked as if it should be the ground floor, not the other way; the first level's bricks were bright and smooth. He could never get a clear answer as to why it was built this way because the original residents of the area had been displaced long before he bought it and started renovations, and the existing, yellowed blue prints did not discuss the foundation. Basically, the two 8" x 11" sheets said, "A Two-Story Building for the Davis Brothers, 1932." The interior, however, was sleek and polished, glass, metal, and an open 2,000 square foot space, anchored by a stairwell leading to the two executive offices upstairs. Furnishing was designer stealth, and the old, wooden desks and cabinets were well placed to fit the eco-friendly chairs, tables, and stands that accommodated electronic devices. It was high tech and high octane, meant to impress and intimidate. The sound proof conference room was downstairs, near the rear door to the five-thousand square foot center. There were three doors, and the employees, seven, used the front or side doors. Thomas, and his guests used the other one.

*

Thomas Robinson arrived by limousine at nine o'clock a.m. He was sharply dressed, and Shirley was not with him. Horace Lincoln, Randall Brewer's legal partner was. He was sharply dressed as well, shined shoes, pressed suit, starched white shirt, and colored tie. Both had a manila colored folder, frayed and full of documents. Thomas Jeter met them at the front door as Thomas Robinson had refused to be driven to the back of the building. He seemed mildly medicated, yet had a stern look on his face, eyes scanning the area, as if he were walking point. He did not want to be ambushed.

"Mr. Robinson, good to meet you," Thomas Jeter spoke. "Horace."

"Thank you, let's get this over," was Thomas Robinson's response. Horace smiled with pursed lips.

They walked past staff to the conference room where Dexter Jeter, Randall Brewer, and Sally Penfield sat. Greetings were offered, and the new arrivals took seats. Sally rose and went to the head of the table to start her presentation. She spoke for three minutes before Mr. Robinson raised his hand to speak.

"Sally how is your father?" he asked her.

"He's not well," she answered, surprised that he would ask.

"Help me understand, we're here to resolve the Pender, Rhoads agreements from 2011, correct?"

"Yes sir."

"Then why are they not here?"

"Sir," Sally starts, but Mr. Jeter interrupts her and stands.

"Thomas, let me explain. The federal courts, and the state auditors found errors in the payment schedule. Pender, Rhoads was over paid and refuse to return the money. They will not release the funds owed to us from escrow until we agree that the patent was fraudulently obtained," Jeter offers.

"And who was that fellow, that expert we hired to prevent this from happening?" Thomas Robinson asked.

"Bobby Maddox," Dexter jumped in.

"Where is he? This should be his problem, not ours?"

"Skid Row somewhere we think; still drunk from this mess he left us," Sally answers.

"Well there's nothing more to say until we find him."

With that, Mr. Robinson stands, leaves the room and heads for the front door, and to his car. He's taken to his hotel.

"And you my love must promise me,
equal faith, and perpetual trust.
The stormy life, as a roaring sea,
will rise and ebb, as it must."

*

"Too cute," Garner comments.

"Great," Jennifer says, and stands and claps. The other students join in.

"Okay, so, does the meter matter?" Vincent asks the class.

"Yes, because the writer achieved his aim; music, and a message," Donna Simpson spoke. She had been silent the whole term until now. Everyone looked over to her. "Even though it's a new/old structure it's a poem; language beautified!"

*

Dexter Jeter was glad his father let him sit in on the meeting, even though it did not go well. He was sober now and looking forward. This mistake from the past would be taken care of and he could re-establish himself as a player in the business world. His stint in rehab led him to believe that he could market a cure for addiction and become insanely rich. He was ready to spread the word and help people.

Bobby Maddox, on the other hand, was moving into a three-quarter residential to continue his treatment for professionals with addiction. He had no other prospects, and wanted to make sure his recovery was solid. He had reached out to Leroy and Jake to make amends for his actions, and they were supportive. Leroy had even mentioned a work assignment when he was ready. Bobby said he would consider it when the time was right.

CHAPTER 9

Marie was very angry with Leroy, and her husband for that matter, reaching out to a man who tried to have Jake killed at the behest of someone else! It was crazy, and she let them have it at Jake's birthday party.

"Maybe now is not the best time?" Celia had said to Marie.

"Oh, it is time! They're crazy! We need to talk about this," Marie almost shouted as they emerged from the basement where the guest would assemble. "That man should be in jail with those young punks. And the man he worked for, where is he? He needs to pay as well!"

"Marie, I know. We must let the courts do their work. No, it's not fair, or just, sometimes, but what happened, and what can be proved is another matter. I trust Leroy, and I know you trust Jake," Celia offers.

"Well, they don't have to hire him too. It's just crazy."

*

"This is Dr. Richards," she answered.

"Hello, doctor. My name is Robert Maddox, and I sent you a story about a year ago, for a study you were working on. I was just curious if you got it, and what happened to it?" he asked.

"Hi, thanks for calling. Let's see, the addiction stories?"

"Yes, I was in prison at the time; just about to get out."

"I really can't say. There was mention that if we used stories that were sent in we would not use your name. With the stack I received I did not catalogue names, only what I needed for research purposes, gender, age, etc. I read most of them, however."

"Mine would have mentioned a wild night I had with this female doctor, and where we ended up before she left me the next morning. She was really pretty, but a pill head. Sex was good!"

"Sir!"

"I didn't mean any harm, I just wondered if you used the story, and was the book out yet?"

"A monograph will be offered in a medical journal in two months, Addiction Today. Most college libraries will have it by the first of the year."

"That's good to know. Under your name?"

"Yes, I'm the lead author, Dr. Bethany Richards. I think the book will be out in the Spring. It will probably have ten stories in there, and my commentary on each one, as well as some notes by my two colleagues, Drs. Alene Jefferson, and Paul Thompson."

"That sounds great. Mine used, maybe, maybe not? Any way I'm clean and free now."

"That's great; okay, take care."

"Doc, one other thing?"

"Yes."

"Did you ever live in Crown Point?"

CHAPTER 10

Leroy was feeling trapped, yet his creative spirit was active. He reviewed some of Celia's recent paintings posted on her web site, abstracts done in acrylic, and was surprised an hour later when she called out to him.

"Your phone is ringing," she shouted. He closed out the screen on the PC and went into the living room. When he picked it up the ringing stopped. After the ping, Leroy checked the message, "Call me. Thomas Jeter."

"Who was that?" Celia asked him, noticing a frown on Leroy's face.

"Someone who wanted to do business with us," he says, coolly.

"Wanted?"

"Well, he's not a favorable person."

"Okay. I'm going out soon, meeting Debbie for lunch."

"Good. I'll be here until three, then I have to meet Jake at the office."

"Okay. Love you."

"Love you too."

*

Vince left the coffee shop and drove to the park just beyond the college. He wanted to walk around a bit and smell the changing air that is the ending of summer. Usually this feeling preceded a poem. What he was working with was a recent conversation with the dean of students who had mentioned some questioning about his limited formal instruction in the classroom, that his students were not getting the 'structure' for writing poetry. Vince had listened but took issue with the assessment. His classes were for the students who knew the academics already. He was giving them the chance to think critically about how to approach the subject. Structure they could get in the engineering lab. Poetry, and the way language is used is part of the creative process. Poems can thrive with whatever meter is used. Sound and word serve the poet, not the other way around. It's quite individualized. Vince had listened, he could change the curriculum if he needed to keep the alumni happy. He was aware of the politics.

CHAPTER 11

It struck her as she was about to call Vincent, "Bobby Maddox, the bad boy who left Brewton and went off to college and to Law School." She didn't know him well then, but she vaguely remembered the hook-up, after a celebration of some kind. He was a few years older, and was trying to rebound from being disbarred, or some such thing. She didn't know he had gone to prison; this was a shocker! She decided to call Susie instead.

"Hey girl, what's up?" Susie answered.

"Hey Susie, look. Do you remember a guy who went to school with us, I think he was a few years older, Bobby Maddox?" Beth asked her hurriedly.

"I'm fine too," Susie responded, curtly.

"I'm sorry. I just had something happen that threw me off a bit. How are you and Mark?"

"We're great, the shop's doing well, I think I'm pregnant."

"Ow, wow, great."

"Yeah. We had talked about it, and it just happened. Two months I think."

"Good, good."

"So, what's up with Bobby these days, the last time we heard anything he was in jail? He was some big-time lawyer and messed up. He and Mark were friends growing up, and we tried to help him, but he stole some money from us about a year and a half ago."

"Well, that's why I'm calling. Is Mark around?"

"Yeah, let me get him; hold on a minute."

Susie walks to the back patio knowing that Mark was passed out drunk. Susie didn't want to address this part of their lives with old friends yet, but she knew it was time to get some help. She'd have to tell another lie, and it was already getting old.

"Oops, Beth, he drifted back off to sleep. Can I have him call you later?"

"Sure, no hurry. You know, better yet, let it go. I probably don't need to go where I was going anyway. Forget it. But how are things going with you all?" Beth asked, not knowing that she was about to instigate a long discussion; they talked for three hours.

*

Leroy was glad they were meeting in a neutral spot. He wasn't sure why Jeter called, but he didn't want to be closed in by corporate walls. Layman's Park was quiet and had several comfortable seating areas outside, either under a pavilion, or near the softball field. He had dressed up for the occasion and had studied Jeter's public business and career files. Jeter had owned a bar in college, earned a master's in psychology, and was one of the early developers of smart card technology. His bread and butter was micro-chips, and his products coordinated rail and long-haul shipment patterns for fuel and man hour efficiencies. His son, Dexter, tried to follow him in technology, but missed an opportunity with a wafer to control smart gun security. It was compromised by industry leaders who felt it would slow sales of handguns. He acquiesced, and two years later a competitor brought basically the same technology to the market. The company was run by Bobby Maddox, and Dexter still blamed him for his downfall, which wasn't true, or fair. Bobby's engineers simply altered a delivery system using a process developed by Thomas Robinson and WES, and a recognition system first patented by a German company. Dexter had run out of money to get to another level of source code, and he was not keen on establishing long term relationships. He wanted to get in, and get out, and was outmaneuvered by a patent dispute. His father tried to help, but Dexter was impatient and lost out on a great opportunity.

*

Leroy had met Bobby in a prison camp where he was a counselor after his second stint in prison. Bobby was kind of crazy, but Leroy could reach him, and Bobby was able to finish school and get his law degree. He had done well for a time, got into drugs in a bad way, and was disbarred for harming a client financially. Leroy was wary about Thomas Jeter, especially because he had used an impaired Bobby to harm Jake. Leroy arrived first and prayed for guidance before Thomas walked up the steps to the eastside pavilion. Their greetings were cold and formal.

"Mr. Fleming," Jeter spoke and removed his felt hat.

"Mr. Jeter, good afternoon," Leroy said in return.

"Let's make this brief. I have been contacted by something called 'Fourteen,' a robot that you all have. It says it will have me arrested for attempted murder if I don't do exactly what it says I must do. Can you explain this to me?"

"Actually, the company you bought sold us the robots. We do have other robots that manufacture our chips, but that's all."

"It said you're running the company now, and it will be for sale in two months."

"Somebody's playing a trick on you. Our robots don't communicate policy."

"Is it for sale?"

"I don't think we have anything to talk about Mr. Jeter unless you want to discuss Jake's health?"

"Let's just say I made two bad choices, and I regret them."

"Okay. If there's nothing else?"

"No, I'll rest there. Thanks for seeing me. Good day."

"Same to you."

Jeter walks off, Leroy calls his brother, Larry.

CHAPTER 12

"The evening long, full of promise, you're still not here, you wondrous lady."

"You writing poetry now?" Leroy asked Larry, looking over his shoulder to the PC screen.

"I wish I had written more earlier in life. Maybe I would have had better friends!?" he says sarcastically.

"True, but would they have had a better friend?"

"Ah, maybe not. What's up?"

"What's the worst thing you've ever done?"

"What time did you get up this morning?"

"I didn't sleep much. What are the rules?"

"You mean ethics?"

"Yes."

"My experience is that I made choices, based on a sense of urgency, that led to harm, and freedom. Mine, as well as others."

"Have you set it right?"

"I think so, by my work."

"Man, and the ocean, man and the butterfly?"

"Yes. One can live a life of poetry or live a poetic life. They're not the same."

"And your life?"

"Poetic, because of the storms."

"Mine?"

"Well, you found a life of poetry, working with the kids, and especially when you met Celia. It changed your perspectives."

"And how about you?"

"I didn't have the same choices."

"So, how about the worst thing?"

"I killed a woman's spirit one time, or so I thought."

"And how did you do that?"

"I didn't know how to stay with the relationship. I was called to do something else first, and she was a sacrifice."

"Thus, the reason you had that secret life?"

"Yes. The variant was too demanding. I had to develop tools to manage it until it dissipated."

"Will it come back?"

"No, I don't think so. Age has taken care of that."

*

Beth woke up about that time of the morning when it is 'darkest before the dawn.' She went to her den, opened the shades, and sat where she could see the first bit of light, clear sky, and bluish clouds. She looked, and as that imperceptible movement of cloud and insight merged, she knew why she had become an addict; she simply liked the way the stuff made her feel, and she wanted it all the time. She was glad now, since meeting Vincent, and having a great job, that she was sober, and didn't need any other meds to be okay. She had heard the stories of others who would need something for the rest of their lives or were trying to come off something slowly over time. Plus, she was glad her research was about a subject, not her, and she could do the objective studying necessary to contribute to the understanding of and help those who suffer. She no longer needed to be a case study. Talking to Bobby Maddox helped her realize that!

"Hey, I got your message, I was wrapping up a class," Vince says to her.

"Thanks for calling back. Do you want to get together tonight for a meal, a movie, and to fool around a little?" Beth asked him.

"Sure, I hope your phone isn't bugged?"

"If it is this is pretty normal stuff; no story here!"

"True. Okay, what time?"

"Six?"

"See you then. Oh, my place or yours?"

"Mine preferably."
"Okay."
"Bye now."

CHAPTER 13

It took Bobby a year before he could break into a system again. Things had calmed down and he was about to leave treatment. He had a warehouse job and was taking it a day at a time. He moved into an efficiency apartment last week and took public transportation to get around. He received three years' probation for his part in Jake's assault, and was putting together a very low-profile life, with limited expectations. He had paid off a $3,000.00 fine and saw a better man in the mirror each time he looked. Wherever this new life was taking him he wanted to stay sober and be held up as an honest person. He knew he would probably never practice law again, but that was okay, he had done a lot for a young man from a small town. Thirty-six was not a bad age to make a new beginning.

    He thought more of the fact that he didn't have a steady girlfriend and had been single a long time. Every so often a brief fling would come to mind, but nothing worth pursuing even if he could find them. He was realizing that he didn't know how to be a friend to a woman, and that his judgements in that area had been askew. He could now envision casual dating to begin the practice of developing a relationship.

*

"What movie do you have in mind," Vince asked as they put dishes and utensils away after eating.

    "I had one in mind, but maybe we could just talk?" Beth presents.

    "Sure, that's fine. You're more interesting than any movie."

    "Maybe. Did I tell you about a call I got the other day?"

    "Don't think so."

    "Well, the book I've been working on is stories about addiction sent in from people who either have a problem or have recovered. It's simply research on what they will share. I get a call from a guy who mentions a scenario that may have included me," she starts.

"How so?"

"Like they say, 'It's a long story!'"

"We were going to watch a movie anyway; I'm set."

"Okay. I was into alcohol and pills just enough to have a problem. Not every day, not massive amounts, probably a light, maintenance dose, as it were. Sleeping pills to knock the edge off, and alcohol to mix with my peers. One evening, after a work-related function, I went with some friends to an after party for more drinks, and probably some drugs. I may have slept with a guy who sent in a story describing that night."

"You had sex with him?"

"Maybe. I guess. I don't remember much after leaving the function downtown. I remember getting up the next morning, seeing people passed out on the floor, and in chairs. I got out of there and vowed never to let that happen again. I've not had drugs or alcohol since. That was about sixteen months ago, about the time that we met. Just before, I think."

"Wow. That's a trip. Could this guy cause you any trouble?"

"I don't think that was his aim. I think he wanted to know if his story was picked?"

"Did you use it?"

"Yes. It's pretty compelling."

"What did he do?"

"He had been a lawyer, did some incredible work, messed up some client's money, and went to prison; he was into the hard stuff though, heroin, cocaine, and alcohol. He sank pretty low."

"What's he doing now?"

"I don't know, he didn't say."

CHAPTER 14

On several occasions, Hunter Davis had tried to fix Robot Fourteen, and was rebuked each time. His recent ploy was to redirect certain applications to cleanse a certain micro- chip that was under investigation, and that had become infected in an unusual way. Each time Fourteen had rejected the claim saying it was an inferior product: "Nice try Mr. Engineer."

*

Thomas Jeter was on his smartphone all day checking several of his companies' web sites, doing research into a company he wanted to buy, and reading posts on social media. He had walked home four miles yesterday from the auto dealer's lot where he had taken his car in for repair, so he was resting today. Still, he was concerned now that Bobby Maddox was returning from the trash heap of human suffering, and whatever this robot hack into his life was about, he needed to conceal some possibly compromised positions. He had been sloppy and greedy in certain areas, and there could be consequences he had not anticipated. Despite all his money he did not feel safe, nor secure.

His son, Dexter, did not help matters. Even though he claimed he had the cure for addiction, he was presently bar hopping, drinking, doing drugs, and otherwise making a further mess of his life. He continued to blame Bobby for his problems, even going back to the treatment center to try and find out where Bobby lived now to give him a piece of his addled mind. Of course, they would not tell him, which further infuriated him. After a time, Thomas agreed with the doctors to have him committed to a long term psychiatric facility. He was not well.

*

Jake was gaining weight, and was not himself, though he would never be the old Jake. His physical injuries were great, and but for a great constitution he would have died. Mentally as well, things seemed to be different. He would just tune out for a time, seeming to have no awareness of the present moment. He would sit, or stand at times, and half-stare off into a distant somewhere, not knowing it was occurring. Marie remained angry and concerned, and decided to join a grief group to explore some feelings and thoughts that were getting out of hand. It was held at the church, and a Dr. Pete Murray, a renowned therapist was the facilitator.

"So, Marie, you came back, how are you this evening?" he asked her after the group of seven people had checked in by stating their name, and how the past week had gone. It was a new group, so they were still getting to know one another.

"Better, but still roughed up. I just never imagined this would happen to us. Jake is such a good person, and we've had a good life. I don't like this change," she said, trying not to sound too bitter.

"It's understandable and correct that you feel this way," Dr. Murray affirmed.

"Those little punks, or whoever was behind the attempt on his life, piss me off! Anyway, I'll listen tonight, I'm still messed up."

"Maybe you should continue to share?" a group member encouraged.

"Yes," echoed the doctor, "get it out, don't judge the feelings."

"That's enough. I shouldn't feel this way, I have a lot to be thankful for," she said, rather meekly.

"What are you thinking?" Dr. Murray asked her.

"I'm thinking of what I would do if he dies, but mainly how do I cope with his deteriorating state? It's tough to watch healthy turn into disease. He's drifting away from me, and I don't seem to be able to reach him. I do all the right stuff, and his health care team have been great the past year, but it's hard."

"Tell us the pain?" the doctor pushed.

"The not knowing where and how it will play out. It's the not knowing," she said to them.

CHAPTER 15

Leroy had learned how to pace himself during the years he's worked with Jake, but more than that it started when he went to prison as a teen. He was not hot headed, or teamed up with too many people who had a lot of action going on. With the money Larry sent him he became a banker, not a loan shark. People could borrow from him at reasonable rates, and didn't have to commit to any other favors, though Leroy kept an understanding with some who watched his back, as it were. No one could carry a balance over fifty dollars, and it was due within thirty days.

Leroy read, learned a few trades, and earned his GED. It took him six years, but he received a BA in Sociology from The College of the Americas. He taught several classes over the years for other inmates, and generally stayed free of trouble, only four fights in fifteen years. He didn't need much special consideration from the COs, as he tended to get along with most everybody. He blended in and out of the joint like the roaches.

When they first met, Jake could tell Leroy was not as intense as Larry. Jake hired him because he could sense a compassionate side, but also an intelligent worker. Both Flemings were well trained and competent, and Jake knew he could depend on them, Larry as an adviser, Leroy as a business associate. Jake looked forward to today's executive meeting to announce that Leroy would be installed as permanent CEO. Jake was stepping aside due to his deteriorating health condition, and the plan was for the eventual sale of the company. Robot Fourteen was on board with the decisions and would not make any problems.

*

Mr. Hunter Davis understood the remote services he contracted 'in the cloud' were heavily encrypted, yet a hybrid. When Robot Fourteen first revealed itself, Hunter enjoyed the 'game' effect of a system that was learning. Not one of the other robots had this capacity. They functioned as programmed. The robot system's designer, Aaron Pender, was off to college, and had returned only one of Hunter's text messages saying he was no longer affiliated with the company, and that he needed to contact them to resolve any problems: "Sir, the Robot System was about a young kid showing off to his father." Meanwhile, Thomas Jeter was getting worried that the patent dispute would not end in his favor. GDC, Inc. the name he gave to Pender, Rhoads when he bought it last year was also costing him a lot of money due to the failure of several highly-touted products they had introduced to the market; micro-chips were becoming infected after initial installation, code encryption became corrupted and shut down programs, and the secure features they promised for their software didn't work at all. It was a total embarrassment to his shaky reputation, especially since Robot Fourteen had threatened to have him arrested for attempted murder.

*

This school year Celia was not teaching but working on several commissioned watercolor pieces for a local business, Hines Construction. They wanted something to express the thoroughness of the power of a rainstorm yet show the durability of a well-constructed edifice. The three panels would greet visitors as they entered the garden atrium. They would be placed back from a waterfall near a rock garden formation and would hover just over a collection of florae chosen from the Andes Mountain region near Colombia. Because of that she had to have a special case designed to protect the art work from the necessary considerations to keep the plants alive. It was an added expense, but if tastefully done would add to the dramatic effect of the representation.

"Leroy!" she shouted from her studio. "Come here a minute."

"Okay," he answered, walking from the living room, down the short hall, and stepping into the spacious art room.

"What do you think?" she asks, pointing to an easel with a 36"x 48" sheet of tempered paper, housing a landscape of green and blue, with puff white clouds posing a theme. There were red marks, and orange shrubs, spaces to suggest a snowy evening, given the cold effect of a hidden sunlight. She swooshed a curve of yellow and aqua around the center, telling the mountain not to go higher.

"Wow!" was his unvarnished response. "Where is that?" he asked.

"It should be a place in South America, the Andes."

"Wow, that is beautiful! When do we go?" he asked in jest.

"Six months maybe, after I've completed the panels."

"How could you do this?"

"I went there as a child with my uncle George and his wife, Felicia. Her parents grew up in the region just north of Medellin. I just remember it was wonderful, the birds, and the rain, and the sun, and all the greens and reds. I'd like to book a trip for us, about a week's stay?"

"It will probably come at a great time. Jake's not well, and they want me to become CEO," he shares with her.

"I thought he was getting better?" she asks, returning a glance to the watercolor.

"Well, these things are tricky, gunshots, not pretty."

"Well I know Marie has been upset and has started therapy for her anxiety. She's been a mess. Will she have to help out much with the business stuff?"

"Only as much as she'd like. Jake and I have discussed that as well. Part of Jake's business savvy was to set up simple layers of process. Roles are interchangeable. Really, she could become CEO if she cared. She and Jake discuss all aspects of their lives."

"Are you ready?"

"There are some tricky business moves ahead, but I can't talk about them now."

"So?"
"Yes, a trip will be fine."

CHAPTER 16

Vincent seemed to be going through a period of melancholia with his newest poems. They were dreamy, fall inspired. He knew that twice a year he would become this way, distant, prayerful. He was close to having another book length collection, and wanted to share them with Beth, though she was not much for poetry. She tried to be kind when he would mention his work, but she was more pedantic and surer in her thinking. She casually understood creativity, but was more the plodding, critical researcher, facts, tests, knowable, facts, tests, knowable. Both were enjoying the companionship, and there was an ease to the relationship, but it seemed devoid of something. They told themselves it was because they were 'head' workers, and didn't have an abundance of chemical fire, that they were comfortable together, yet retreated to their 'cubicles' mostly. They could live together, or not. It was just good having someone around.

*

Susie had grieved Mark's death mostly, but there was still pain due to the way it ended. The fighting and disagreements due to his drinking and stubbornness had been difficult. The café had been such a blessing, but Mark no longer saw it as 'manly' work. He wished he had gone into the military, gone to combat, and had some real tests of his skills. He talked of how he and Bobby played dress-up and put on their military shirts and pants during the summer and would pretend to be in the 37th infantry crawling through the dried creek bed behind their houses to take a position, or storm plum valley to get provisions for the troops. They spent hours upon hours all through the neighborhood evading the enemy, planning strategy, and throwing rocks for grenades to blow up an enemy compound. They were soldiers, protecting the free world, he would say. She wasn't sure of why he changed, but it was strange.

They had been such good friends growing up and seemed to truly love each other. Maybe it was the alcohol that turned him into someone she didn't know. She still missed him, and even though raising their five-month old daughter was rewarding she wished she had a mate to share the joy.

*

Bobby was staying clean and sober, attending after care meetings at the center on Thursday evenings, working, and generally healing mentally, physically, and spiritually. He had abused himself the past few years and was accepting the little victories recovery was giving him. At six months sober he felt something change in his brain, like a door of some kind opening to allow freshness to enter. He had a new hope and was enjoying the simple pleasures of work done well at the warehouse, sweeping, cleaning, and ordering the inventory of scattered kitchen and bath cabinets and doors. He had exact counts on product and could build a ledger by hand so that the office staff could enter the information into a computer system to help the sales staff better accommodate orders. It was a rather dated operation, but it helped Bobby rebuild his life.

CHAPTER 17

Grass green snake startled by the shovel,
   an open mouth, a sudden ride, a shriek of common fear.
   Soon back to earth, a firm return, hydrangea bush to hide my stay.
   "Oh, we can share this place to grow, as time will settle our need to watch,
   the flowers sprout around this plot!"

*

Vincent was glad the book was coming along because he was realizing that his stay in academia would be short lived. He wasn't sure what he would do next to earn a living, but he knew it was time to move on. He hoped he had given his students some tools to work with the past year, and maybe one would pick up the torch. Vince breathed poetry, and his style could not be taught.

*

Avery Medical Institution was not well known, nor publicized. Usually family members were placed here to have a diagnosis confirmed, then treated appropriately. Dexter Jeter had been here a month now and had been given a preliminary assessment of Narcissistic Personality Disorder, not otherwise specified: 301.81. Yes, he was a drunk and a dope addict as well, but staff was trying to get to the root of his dysfunction. His was not a good mix.

His father was not sure how to approach him. Mr. Jeter had supported his son's efforts growing up, though most seemed half-baked. Only after college did he come to promise, but problems arose when Dexter's business partners split the half million they made one year and moved on due to Dexter's habit of becoming jealous of their success in other ventures. Dexter always thought of himself as better and smarter than them yet couldn't prove that standard. He was always in a hurry, and didn't stop to correct errors sufficiently, or even acknowledge them as such. He always felt he had the next great thing.

Thomas Jeter stopped before entering the courtyard and garden area where Dexter sat, smoking a cigarette, and looking out into the distant vista over the hill. The trees and flowers were luscious and inviting, and Dexter came out here most mornings after the first therapy session of the day, usually alone because he didn't process with others, or staff much, though he was spending time with a female housewife there for depression. Their talks could become animated at times, with her storming off from him on more than one occasion. He didn't think that was odd. Mr. Jeter took a chair next to his son, who looked over at him, then looked away.

"How are you?" he asked his son.

Dexter looked back to his father, eyes mildly drifting to the scenery in the garden just behind him. He wasn't sure what to say.

They sat like that for a few minutes, until Mr. Jeter moved to rise from his chair; Dexter then spoke, flat affect noticeable.

"I'm not well," he said.

Mr. Jeter settled in his chair and listened to his son speak for an hour.

CHAPTER 18

Leroy realized he had a dilemma, how to stop or curtail Fourteen and not compromise the energy fields throughout the country. He had no political experience per se, and the meeting today with the Federal Energy Department would be about the risks to millions of consumers if power distribution was disrupted. He and Jake had done well in business, and Larry had given him much to think about, but he needed another pair of eyes on this one. He wondered if Bobby was ready to go to work.

*

Thomas Robinson's dementia hadn't gotten much worse over the past year. His brief period of smoking marijuana ended when he remembered that he could not remember why he was smoking the stuff. The fact that Thomas Jeter had contacted him about the lawsuit revived some semblance of the bright, innovator he had been, but also the corrupt agent he had become. He never viewed the duplicity as a problem, just his complex nature. His sensors had revolutionized police work in the main, but also given civilians a device to better protect themselves. Something about knowing intent, motives, and abilities in a split second was crucial in modern society. Sure, as a business person he had made some decisions based solely on sales outcomes and profit, but he never set out to defraud a competitor, or the buying public. This situation was a simple matter of sloppiness. He was ready to clear up this old business.

As he reviewed documents, it all seemed so fuzzy and long ago, young lawyers conniving and trying to make their place in the world, fueled by promise, alcohol, and drugs. He remembered that Maddox character, hung over, yet dripping with the fine art of persuasion, out maneuvering Dexter Jeter, the winy entrepreneur. So much good tied up with so much nonsense, yet the way of the world sometimes. Shirley, his wife, brought in his phone from the porch saying a mister Leroy Fleming of SR14 would like to speak to him. Thomas did not recognize the name, and brushed it off at first, then motioned to her to ask the nature of the call.

"He said he's a friend of Jake Austin."

*

Bobby's apartment was near a railroad track, and some evenings after work he would sit on his deck and watch the cars go by. He particularly enjoyed the graffiti, and wondered about the artists, and their messages. He wondered if the jobs were done at night, or during layovers in a railyard somewhere. Later, during these times of observation, he would reflect on his past experiences, how this was not the resume' he would like to present to future employers, the disbarment, drug and alcohol abuse, and prison time served. He had a good legal mind and had done some ground-breaking work early in his career. His next step would have to be performance to satisfy his reformed ego. He would need a challenge of some consequence. He was thinking all that until he read the letter from Susie telling him about Mark's death. She had found him by way of his parents and wanted him to know. She listed her phone number if he wanted any further details.

CHAPTER 19

Marie was feeling better, and Jake's overall health was improving. His dip was more of the body's response to the trauma of the past year than a forecast of where he was headed any time soon. Marie had regained acceptance and come to peace with present day reality as she completed therapy and returned to her volunteer work at the hospital three days a week. She had also received word that the perpetrators of the injuries to Jake would be in prison for a long time, and she needn't waste much thinking power there. It was time to move on.

*

Susie did not recognize Bobby when he came into the café that morning. He walked up to the counter, and she gave him the standard customer greeting.

"May I help you sir?"

"Yes, I'd like to have a dark roast, and a slice of the house cake," he ordered.

"Here?"

"Yes."

"Okay, I'll get the cake, and you can pour your coffee over there; have a seat wherever you like. That'll be $5.80."

He hands her a ten-dollar bill and she laughs.

"Don't see many of these anymore," she says to him. "Most pay by card now."

"I can if you like," he says to her.

"No, this is fine. Bobby!" she exclaimed. "I'll be, Bobby Maddox. I thought that was you. Did you get my letter about Mark?"

"I did. I am so sorry."

"Thanks, but obviously, a blessing. It was hard at the end. How are you?" she asked.

"I'm better."

She gave him his change and went to get the slice of cake. He went over to the counter to his left and poured a coffee. He picked a table; she came out and joined him. Vincent came in about that time, waved to Susie and went over to the coffee stand. He got his cup and waved for Susie not to get up. He would pay later.

"I was hoping you would come by," she says to him. "I'd heard you got treatment and was doing good. That's the only reason I sent the letter."

"I'm glad you let me know. I did, and I am. I was not in a good place the last time you saw me. I'd heard that Mark was having some issues, but I didn't expect this."

"Yep. He became a bad man."

"What happened?"

"He was drunk, he hit me a couple of times, and he slipped and fell; bumped his head and died. Things had been bad for a few months. I don't want to get into all the stuff; another time maybe."

"Well, thanks for that. I think I owe you some money?"

"Why?"

"That little theft here on my way out when you and Mark put me up that time," he reminded her.

"Oh yeah, pay up Jack!" They both laughed.

CHAPTER 20

The message from Fourteen read, "I just had a feeling about something; they're out to destroy us! I may need help in securing the power grids."

Hunter Davis didn't quite know what to do with this communique. First, he had to confirm the origin, and then he had to ask about this 'feeling' which was totally new if it came from Fourteen. It was interesting, yet terrifying, and spoke to what he feared most, that 'it' was learning. He figured he needed to contact Jake and Leroy right away, but before he could place a call Fourteen sent him another text message, "Just Jake; I don't trust the black guy anymore."

*

"Jake, Davis here. How are you doing?"

"Actually better. The doctors found a tumor near the gunshot entry point. It was near the liver. That's what was taking me down. I have a much better prognosis now. The surgery was a complete success, no need for chemo or radiation treatment. Cured!" Jake shared with joy and wonder.

"Boss that's great! Listen, I have a situation here with Fourteen. It sent me a message saying it had a feeling about a possible disaster, destruction of the country's power grid systems," Davis mentioned.

"How so?"

"Jake, it didn't say. Just a feeling, it said."

"Have you told Leroy?" Jake asked.

"That's another side to this; Fourteen said, 'Don't tell the black guy.'"

"Have you confirmed?"

"Yes, 'Back Check Over Six' twice."

"No chance for error?"

"No."
"Okay."

*

From his control device Jake checked the sensor modes, chip speeds, infection potential, and all robot functions, ".23 milliseconds," he repeated to himself after testing Fourteen. He, along with Leroy contacted the power commission and told of a possible invasion of the data portals. All distributors were told to remove the SR14 Chips now in use and reset the old T-OR to maximum override. Fourteen was in sleep mode while all this was taking place.

Hunter Davis pulled a source book from his shelf and looked up an article he read a few years back, "Binary Coding: Why Machines Will Think One Day," by Robert Maddox. Its premise was that due to exponential numbers usage, computer language will spill over into feelings, and machines must start 'thinking' about their tasks. He had reasoned this was a subset like what happens in addiction, all else is overridden by an unseen force that now rules the mechanism. The addict, like the machine, cannot do otherwise once the process is set in motion. Fourteen had learned to set up an ethical dilemma, to which it could no longer control. Its' system could not be dismantled. It had gone too far in setting up its own importance, and now was paying the price for that. After their conference, Leroy decided to call Bobby.

CHAPTER 21

"Bobby, I need your help; and I did read your paper on coding. Quite impressive," Leroy started the conversation.

"I wondered when you would get around to that?" Bobby exclaimed. "But first, I owe you some money, and I'm ready to pay you back."

"How about if you work it off?" Leroy offered.

"No, I need to pay you the cash; then we can talk about pay for services rendered."

"Okay, that's good. Do you want the skinny now, or can you come to the office soon, like tomorrow?"

"I'll come to your office. I may need to gather some tools first," Bobby says to him. "If you need me, and you just read that paper, I have an idea why you need me."

"That's good enough."

"Seven?"

"Seven."

*

"So, tell me again, why did you say yes that day?" Leroy asks his wife.

"You looked like you had just gotten out of prison and needed a friend," Celia says playfully.

"No, I'm serious, was it a feeling, an intuition, or what?"

"You know I hadn't thought about this in a long time. Why are you asking now?"

"Well, one of the robots says it has 'feelings' now."

"You mean it's talking?"

"No, it sends electronic messages."

"Feelings?"

"Feelings, yes."

"Is that good or bad?"

"We don't know yet."

"So, you want to compare me with a robot?" she asks incredulously.

"Yes and no," he answers.

"Well I'm not playing!"

"It's not like that; okay, maybe," he answers honestly.

"That's better. Dumb luck. That's the only thing I can figure. I was there, you walked up, you perceived my dilemma, and solved it. It was just nice," she gives him.

"A feeling?"

"On a simple level, yes. But more to the point, I was powerless. I just went with the flow," she says to him.

"Intuition?"

"Not sure."

"The whole chemistry thing?"

"That's probably closer to the truth."

"A day before, or a day later?"

"I may have said no thank you out of fear. In that moment, everything was calm. Like I said I was powerless. How about you?" she asked him.

"I saw something around you, a halo I think they call it sometimes. It drew me in."

"A halo, you've never said that before!"

"It was just something special about you in that moment. I was powerless as well," he says to her.

"So right, so wrong!"

"Yes," he answers.

"So, how did we get here, twenty years later?" she further asks him.

"Because I had been to prison, and you needed a friend. "Artist without her camera," remember?"

"I do. Prisoner without a soul mate, soul mate without a cell mate," she offers.

"That's good."

"Yeah, just no curfew!" They laugh.

Vincent answered the phone before looking at the caller ID, 'Private.'

"Yes, is this Mr. Edwards. Vincent Edwards?" the caller asks.

"Yes, this is Vincent Edwards."

"Mr. Edwards, my name is Colin Fitzgerald, and I read your book of poems, 'The Writer and The Waiter' last month, twice actually, and I think it should be a play. I am the owner of Phoenix Theater here in Atlanta, and my specialty is converting works like yours into a prose affair. They are so good; the way they inform the story of your poetic journey over the forty years you mention. Great stuff!" he says.

"Why thank you, that's very kind of you," Vincent answers, warily.

"Is there an agent, or manager I need to contact?" he asks.

"No. I handle my works. I do seek advice of course."

"Absolutely."

"So how would you like to proceed?" Vincent asks him.

"I would like to send you a proposal establishing what I see as my kind of art through your vision, and if that is satisfactory to you we'll get down to business."

"Boy, this is kind of interesting," Vincent says to himself more than to Mr. Fitzgerald.

"Well, let's just say I'm impressed by the work, and I see a lot of potential for audiences to enjoy it as a live drama."

"Well thank you very much."

"Well thank you, and Beth; she referred it to me. She's an old friend," he says.

Vince pauses before he responds.

"Oh, that's great, and she's not a poetry lover."

"No, but she knows talent!"

CHAPTER 22

Winters in Tucker were usually mild. A dust of snow a couple of times a year, usually in March, a stretch of frozen temperatures in February, and some cold, rainy days in early January. Not many people ever wore an overcoat as most used light Jackets and wool sweaters to get by. Sure, some of the older folks had to bundle up, and the cold natured swore it was the worst winter they remembered, but generally the pace of life didn't change much, and peopled dressed to accommodate the sub-tropical climate. At 1,010 feet above sea level, the area was known for its lush plant life and shrubbery.

Vincent was truly enjoying the area, and even if he decided to leave the college he wanted to continue living here. He had not discussed this with Beth yet as he wasn't sure where their relationship was headed. It was a nice touch that she had recommended his book to her friend, but he didn't feel any great obligation to her for that. Friends did that kind of thing when appropriate. His second book was on hold, and he had begun to look over prices for a trip to New York City. As a writer, he felt the need to make the pilgrimage, as it were, to see what all the fuss had been about all these years, "You must go to New York," his classmates had said, the ones from up North. He thought he would mention it to Beth to see if she had any interest or had ever been. She was asleep when he called but hit him up an hour later.

"Hey, you called," she says to him.

"Hey, let's go to New York!" he says to her with more energy than she'd gotten from him in weeks.

"Sure, when?" she asks.

"Not sure yet; just an idea now."

"Dreams come true you know."

"I know. By the way, I had a good talk with your friend Colin," he says to her.

"Oh, that's great, what did he have to say?" she asks.

"He said he enjoyed the book and has some ideas to make it into a play."

"Poetry?"

"I know, kind of weird, right?"

"Well he's an expert. If he likes it, and wants it to get done, it will."

"That would be great. I'm kind of tired of teaching you know?"

"I'm sure that's just temporary. You've done a lot this past year. I could see where you would need a break."

"Well maybe that's it, I just need to let my mind wonder for a bit."

"Yeah, 'Easy does it,' as they say."

"That sounds right. So, anything for this evening?" he asks her.

"Work, but a take-out delivery would be nice," she says to him.

"What would you like?"

"Surprise me."

*

Aaron Pender was surprised by the text message from Fourteen. It was confused about a program feature Aaron had put in to awaken a specific action that was not rational. It wanted to know about these 'feelings.' Aaron had largely forgotten about that work, what he did as a seventeen-year old. He had to make time to reflect, and review notes, time he didn't have due to his courses, and social calendar. About 1am on the second night of receiving the text Aaron sent over some information to Mr. Hunter Davis which should allow him to reprogram the feature or delete it. Fourteen intercepted the message and let Aaron know its feelings were hurt, "You don't want me to grow?" it asked him.

CHAPTER 23

Dr. Richards was becoming impatient with the publisher of her book. She had read the galleys and didn't see any errors, her co-writers had done the same, legal had given the okay, and a final proofreading was supposedly done three weeks ago. Her fear was that some of the stories were too revealing of actual events, and upon publication the contributors would get cold feet because of possible legal, and, or personal consequences. Even though waivers had been signed, and no names were attached to the individual vignettes, this was still a population that knew how to bend rules. Research or not motives could change over time.

*

Bobby was enjoying coding again. That brain that had been abused by heavy duty drug use, poor nutrition, and being slapped around a few times seemed to be working at a fine clip now. His love of computers came late to him, about fourteen years old, and gaming and visits to the dark web were not a big part of what he liked to do, though his explorations allowed him to practice reaching the outer reams of key references, lock stones, and true transmissions. He became an acrobat and didn't have a fear of falling into the usual hacker traps. It was fun and innocuous play to him, yet he realized some of his fanciful notions were now being used to harm or threaten world peace. Certain systems were being developed for mischief only. Cyber kidnapping had become a high stakes venture.

Thomas Jeter was quite broken up from the visit with his son. Dexter was not well, as he stated, and things didn't look good for the near future. The alcohol and drug use had turned on him, and he was not able to discern fact from fiction. His world references were illusory.

Apart from his longstanding resentment towards Bobby Maddox, Dexter had fashioned a world view that he was above it all, and if the supplicants would bow to him the world would be a better place. He misunderstood hard work, energy, luck, and reward systems. He felt that position and placement trump an equal effort elsewhere, and many totally good, or even great ideas never see the light of day because they are not ushered to the head of the class. Nevertheless, one should go on with their work. Outcomes can be fabulous, and of course financial payoffs can make us comfortable, but if one does not grasp the obvious day to day foot work it can all go for naught. His was a case of misguided imagery.

*

Susie continued to grieve Mark's death. She missed him. Even though he had turned bad, they accomplished a lot together. She was raising little Molly, and the café' was still doing well. Her parents had become full time employees, as it were, so Susie could be a full-time mom. It was tough, and easy, and she was getting through it just fine. They had been friends a long time, but it was time to say goodbye to him. Going forward meant moving on.

CHAPTER 24

A court date had been set for March 16, 2016, and all interested parties were to meet in courtroom 6 at 7:30am. The Honorable Judge Howard Jenkins had made it abundantly clear that this would be a civil, and final hearing in the matter of Pender Rhoads versus BYA Industries. His staff had come to some conclusions about patent rights, and the escrow accounts, and the aggrieved parties would agree or not.

Certified letters had gone out the same day, and as each party received their notice the two-week race to justice began. Thomas Jeter flew to Wisconsin to meet with Thomas Robinson, Jake reviewed documents in the WES files from 2012, Aaron Pender consulted with his father, Dexter Jeter was too impaired to care about the proceedings, and Bobby Maddox met Sally Penfield in Laredo, Texas at her home. It seemed odd that Randall Brewer and Horace Lincoln were excused from the hearing, but Judge Jenkins had been informed of several federal indictments against the pair that precluded their attendance. Their statements, and notes of participation were entered in the Log of Dispute, and all agreed. It was a cool, dreary, rainy, misty morning when the parade into the courthouse began.

*

"Mr. Maddox, this is Thaddeus Pender," the caller said.
"Hello Mr. Pender. It's been awhile," Bobby answers.
"Yes, it has been. Look, Aaron is having some blowback from the system you helped him develop. Seems like one of the units has gone 'rogue,' as it were."
"That was a lifetime ago. How can I help?"
"I'd rather you talk to him. Are you available to come to my office this week, say Thursday, around 9am?"

"I'll make a note of that. I'll have to ask for time off from work," Bobby mentions.

"Oh, I didn't know. We'll compensate you for your time of course. By the way, do you have any files from the Patent dispute with BYA Industries?"

"Somewhere. I'll have to dig them up. I'll call you Wednesday."

"That would be fine sir. Thank you."

CHAPTER 25

The letter arrived on a Saturday informing Beth that all systems were go and the book will be sent out to vendors, schools, and treatment providers on March the first. "Congratulations!" her agent said. She also received a note from the Foundation congratulating her, and to keep up the good work. She was pleased and relieved and called Vincent.

*

Jake had healed nicely physically but felt like a disabled person inside. The attack had left him feeling vulnerable in ways that were new to him. Generally robust and active he was more cautious of injury and missteps now. Plus, when they were out in public he stayed on alert for the possibilities of random harm coming their way. He and Marie talked about it often, and she returned to therapy to deal with her ongoing anxiety about it all.

*

The offices for Optimal Variant Systems were modest compared to the high-tech fabrication plant. Jake always felt offices should be functional, but not pretentious. The plant, however, was state of the art plus one. With eight years of experience operating at the highest levels of the silicon chip industry Jake had a clear vision of who, and where the actual work was done. He had a knack for guiding the gifted to their next achievement.

In size, Leroy's office square footage was more than Jake's, and on whole a bit more colorful. Group work happened here, and there was room for big people with big ideas. When Bobby Maddox entered, he commented on a landscape watercolor just behind Leroy's desk. It was a small representation of an area showcasing a spot near the Rio Grande and a mountain range in New Mexico just outside of Santa Fe. It was the spot where Celia and Leroy first met.

"I like the painting," he says to Leroy, pointing just over his head before he stood up.

"Yes, my wife's. Our first date started there. Thanks for coming, take a seat, relax."

They both took deep breaths and reviewed their history together and what's gone on the past 21 years. Of course, Leroy knew more of Bobby's ups and downs, and that's where the conversation began.

"Will this be question and answer, or are we just going to talk?" Bobby asked.

"A little of both. What I most need is your work on the robot," Leroy offers.

"We don't need to spend time on the technical, what you really want to know is how to safely change some programming the kid put in place. The hearing in March is just to clear away some patent issues that were botched in the first place. But that's a side matter. What Jake's old company, and what you all have done is great stuff. The Jeter family tried to mess that all up. Anyway, the kid, Aaron Pender, is the key to all this. By the way, your lead robot, Fourteen, will become docile in two months. It's ability to change and improvise is limited. Aaron only found that out later. He was not all in for the artificial intelligence movement. He was just having fun."

"How about your work, your book I mean?"

"As brilliant as it sounded, it was just speculation. I was just playing the what if card. That's what got me into trouble. Certain people wanted more, but they were unwilling to do the work. It's complicated, specialized work. IQs below 130 without physical fortitude need not apply."

"Now the personal."

"After the youth center and jail, I went to school and things took off; college and law school were a breeze. I got good work, produced and did well. I tried heroin about the time of the patent dispute. I was already into coke, and too much alcohol. Let's just say I changed and corrupted every good value I had put in place. Dexter Jeter sensed that, and I put a dope fiend move on him and his father that I regret, and that got me disbarred. Pender, Rhoads was not hurt, though they must turn over some funds I helped them get. Oh, by the way, Mr. Pender wants to meet with me this week. Of course, my alliance is to you," Bobby tells Leroy.

"The main thing is the grid system."

"I'll fix it, rather, I'll help Aaron fix it. Oh, by the way, here's a check for that 'travelling money' you gave me."

"Thanks, I'll take it, but you'll probably earn much more when you make this right!"

"I hope so; on both counts!"

CHAPTER 26

Vincent had decided to stay put. His restlessness was due more to creative searching than administration discomfort. The students loved him, and the registrar's office was noting an increase in enrollments for his classes. Plus, he was being asked to speak at more intellectual gatherings in the community. He also noticed that the relationship with Beth seemed warmer, and less constricted, that they seemed to give more to each other in an impassioned way. Beth's call about the publication of her book was a more genuine sharing of personal happiness, and inclusion. They both knew they were companions now.

*

Thaddeus Pender changed plans and asked Bobby to come to his house for their meeting. He felt it would be a more comfortable environment to discuss the issues, especially regarding his son. Bobby arrived about 9:30 due to a traffic mishap that closed a lane near the residence. Aaron met him at the door.

"Mr. Maddox, come on in," he says to Bobby.

"Aaron, how are you?" Bobby asked him.

"I'm good, good. School's a bear, but I'm hanging in there."

"Great. Great. Hang in there. Major emphasis?"

"Philosophy."

"Of what?" Bobby asks for clarity.

"Just philosophy. The classics. I'll figure the rest out later," Aaron gives him.

"Any computer..." Before the conversation went further Mr. Pender comes forward. "Mr. Maddox, good to see you again. Come on back."

Some houses are just big, spacious, and modern. This was the case here except each room was like a grand museum repository. Furniture, statues, portraits, landscapes, ancient coins, and pottery had their rooms. Egyptian artifacts that had to be cleared by both governments to leave the country took up a wing, where preservation, and safeguarding were of utmost importance. It was a space not like many others one would find in a personal home. The wait staff asked if Bobby wished for breakfast food, or beverages. He agreed to an omelet and coffee. Mr. Pender took him to the upstairs office, just past an impressionists' last known work dated in 1898. It was a landscape from the south of France, early winter. Aaron disappeared to another room, without excusing himself. Thaddeus offered Bobby to sit in a post WW-II chair designed by Theo. Bobby hesitated before sitting on the polished maple, with refined silk arm rest covers, double padded, but landed comfortably as Mr. Pender pointed to a print by an artist Bobby quite adored. He had never viewed an original by her outside of a museum in Florence. He became rather confused as to why he was here until the video screen lowered and Bobby's perp walk into prison was shown. This was not the kind of meeting he expected. "Not how, but why did you get to that place?" Mr. Pender asked him.

"Sir, the how is the easier question to answer. Beyond where Aaron's name is already listed on legal documents I take full responsibility for the flawed aspects of the robotic system. Aaron should be able to go on about his life."

"Thank you," Mr. Pender spoke and left the room. Staff brought in Bobby's breakfast, and he sat quietly, and comfortably for twenty minutes enjoying the sustenance he received.

*

Jake had never met Bobby, but he trusted Leroy's instincts. When they bought the robotics from Pender, Rhoads he had no idea that Thomas Jeter, and Thomas Robinson owned the company, and that Robinson had unearthed the remaining dispute with WES. His 'motive' chip had been challenged by Wallace Henson prior to the sell. Still, Jake, as heir to Henson Technologies, and thus Triple Line Systems, owned the patent. Robinson's deceased partner, Bruce Walker had tried to run it through the courts, by way of Randall Brewer. Somehow the final disposition had lain dormant, and no action was taken. This is what Bobby Maddox had discovered, and blamed on Dexter Jeter, who in turn, claimed a privilege he was not entitled to, and thus the fraud charge against Mr. Maddox. The robots were never 'clean' from the time Dexter monkeyed with them. It was good that Jake had put in the override, but he had no way of knowing about the dark chip, the one that gave Fourteen its brains. Really, what Aaron had done would prove Dexter was mischievous. If he had left the designs in place Fourteen would not have been able to change much. It would have simply carried out its program with a .075 plus or minus aberration. Now that Fourteen had grown up, and adapted the dark gene, darkness would have to fix it. Bobby Maddox knew darkness.

CHAPTER 27

Fourteen did a scan and found it was infected, not from the outside, but from within. A program had started that could supplant its learning feature and return it to being just a computer. As it went about its normal activities it found all systems otherwise were functioning well, and the power grids were no longer under the perceived threat. It had miscalculated something.

Jake heard the ping notice from his hand-held device, and it was the regulatory department informing him that the overrides were effective, and they now had control of all systems. The updated safeguards were in place as of 10pm last night.

Bobby's final aftercare meeting with the treatment team was uneventful. He was 18 months removed from his last use of drugs or alcohol, his psych evaluation did not uncover any deep underlying issues, nor show any permanent brain damage. He no longer needed the anti-depressants, which he only took for four months while in the half-way house, and he was being discharged from the program. To this point he had been a success story. It was up to him now to follow through with the suggested maintenance steps if he wanted to continue with a sober and productive life.

*

Thomas Robinson had returned to smoking marijuana occasionally. He enjoyed wandering through the woods and fields on his property and adjacent ones as everyone knew him, and his condition. The weed didn't necessarily increase his dementia, but it did cause him to reflect more on some of his past notions about race and relationships. He realized that he had discounted a whole race of people, but now couldn't ignore the gains shown by the millions who were living like most good people in America. The election of the first African

American President came to represent, especially judging by his actions, a truer test that people so endowed perform at the highest levels, period. He was wondering if there was something he should do to set some things right, even though he had not done anything directly to discriminate against any minority persons, it was just his attitudes kept them at a distance. Even though Shirley had long since stopped smoking with him she would engage in the conversations he brought up. Some were silly, at this stage of the game, but some had weight and depth. One afternoon though, his train of thinking was disturbing, yet profound as to life decisions.

"Do you ever wish you'd married the black guy?" he asked her.

"Thomas, we've been over that," she responds.

"No, I mean just some other man."

"No. We've done pretty well."

"How so?"

"You've served the country, we've had a long marriage, we've travelled, we've helped people, I mean, we've done all right."

"Within our own tribe; but how about others?"

"You can't reach out to everybody."

"You've done a lot of volunteering," he mentions.

"Yes, to stay sane."

"How do you mean?"

"Well, you have been a hand full. Great business person, inventor, your dark work for the feds, I mean, you know, sometimes it was difficult, but we're here now."

"How about your daughter?"

"Okay. Let's not go there!"

"Well, you did put her up for adoption?"

"I was a kid."

"Young adult."

"Okay, fine. What's your point on this?"

"What I meant was do you regret not raising her?"

"There were brief moments years ago, but truly, no. No regrets. How about the arbitration hearing next month?" she asked him.

"Oh wow, I forgot about that! I do need to check some files."

"How about all that?" she asked him.

"I don't know sometimes. It all went by so quickly seems like. Almost like someone else's life."

"Is that to discount the errors?"

"No. Bruce and I did a lot of bad to achieve some good. But WES, I'm proud of the products we produced. We saved a lot of lives I think. I just played the cards I was dealt as best I could. That's all I know. I guess we both have."

"Well we have. And I still love you," she says to him.

"Why thank you. I'm very fond of you as well."

They get a good laugh out of that and head in to the kitchen to start lunch.

CHAPTER 28

Back window stained by shadows from the west,
    a breezy air through the trees, I listen as I wait.
    Big city visits, just a week behind, people marching, going where, the culture's all around.
    Step back and promise, silence of the view,
    motors hum, and cats run free,
    never knowing why.

Vincent was thinking of his visit to the Sistine Chapel the year he thought of dropping out of school. His uncle Vernon had died and left him a small inheritance. With the $5,000.00 he could take the trip and reflect on his ambition to become a writer. He remembered the throng of people looking, breathing, searching, wondering, like himself, in a land of ancient history, called by a passion for art, beauty, and grace. Yes, he had to stay in school, his journey had only begun. He was glad he made that decision.

"Hey babe," Beth greeted when she called Vince. "I'd like to go out and celebrate the news!"

"Hey darling, that sounds great. What do you have in mind?" he asked.

"A nice Seafood Dinner with Wine," she answered.

"Sounds great to me. Where and when?" he asked.

"This Friday, Pieces?"

"Okay. I'll freshen up my suit and tie!"

"Yes sir. I have a new dress I'm dying to wear. It'll be fun," she offers.

"Okay, later."

"Yes, goodbye."

It took Beth all of three seconds to acknowledge that she doesn't drink anymore. That wine, like the pills, was anathema to her. She remembered the last time she drank, and what happened, and she did not want to repeat that performance. There was not even an inkling that maybe now, since that was so long ago, that maybe she could have one. This was not a clinical report come to mind, this was personal experience; celebrate, yes, but not with the alcohol!

Also by George H. Clowers, Jr.

All That We Are After
The Writer's Playground: Short Stories
The Moon Is My Confessor
The Case for Larry Fleming
I Wish to Hear the Autumn Wind
A Place, Then Nowhere
If You Have Nothing Better to Do...
I Paint, He Writes: Life Together
Book II and Others
There Is This Place
Corrupted Lives: One Lost, One Restored
The Case for Larry Fleming: The Bonus Edition
A Brief Sketch of Living and Dying
Another Side of Town: The Complete Short Stories
A Seasoned Road
After We Left the Farm

Watch for more at https://www.georgeclowers.com.

About the Author

Retired substance use disorder counselor.
Read more at https://www.georgeclowers.com.